Not Over You

A Prosperity Ranch Novel

Not Over You

A Prosperity Ranch Novel

Heather B. Moore

Mirror Press

Copyright © 2020 by Heather B. Moore
Print edition
All rights reserved

No part of this book may be reproduced in any form whatsoever without prior written permission of the publisher, except in the case of brief passages embodied in critical reviews and articles. This is a work of fiction. The characters, names, incidents, places, and dialogue are products of the author's imagination and are not to be construed as real.
Interior design by Cora Johnson
Edited by JL Editing Services and Lisa Shepherd
Cover design by Rachael Anderson
Cover image credit: Deposit Photos #188545972
Published by Mirror Press, LLC
ISBN: 978-1-952611-01-8

PROSPERITY RANCH SERIES

One Summer Day
Steal My Heart
Not Over You
Seasoned with Love
Take a Chance

Not Over You

He left her behind. She's spent years ignoring him. But some things can never be forgotten.

Knox Prosper knows he can never go back in time and correct his mistakes, so he has to find a way to move forward, and start a new life. Become a better man, and a father, if only for his young daughter. His regrets have taught him to simplify and to focus on what's real and important. Returning to his hometown to ride in the rodeo gives him a chance to spend time with his daughter and to continue mending bridges with the rest of his family. But what he doesn't expect is to run into Jana Harris, the first woman he loved—the woman who faded from his life years before because Knox continued to mess up one thing after another. Someone as good and as sweet as Jana is the last person he deserves. Hope is dangerous. And hope can break his heart once again. Yet, Jana might be the one person with the power to redeem his past once and for all.

1

Dear Miss Jewel,

My boyfriend of three years still hasn't proposed, and now he wants me to move in with him. Should I tell him to put a ring on it?

Sincerely,
Nina, confused in Dallas

Dear Nina,
Three years? You've been patient long enough, honey. It's time to give him that ultimatum. Tell him where you stand. Demand that he meet you halfway in this relationship. If he doesn't, then it's his loss, and you'll be moving on to better things.

Jana Harris backspaced on the entire paragraph, then took another sip of her lemon tea as she read through Nina's plight again. Sometimes, Jana's first response wasn't the best one.

Dear Nina,
There comes a time in every relationship when we need to give the ultimatum, but you need to be able to live with

those consequences, whatever that might be. If three years with no ring is your threshold, then yes, it's time. Have that talk, dear. Let him know that you have hopes and dreams, too.
Rooting for you,
Miss Jewel

There. The relationship advice was solid and genuine, and wouldn't seem pushy to the hundreds of thousands of readers out there. Jana's relationship advice column was syndicated in every major newspaper in Texas, a huge feat if she considered that she operated out of the tiny town of Prosper, and hadn't dated anyone seriously in . . . years.

It wasn't like she didn't want to date. Heck, she was at Racoons, the town bar, every weekend with her besties Patsy and Barb. Jana flirted, laughed, batted her eyes, and danced. Yet . . .

No one was like *him*. And no one would ever be. That was okay, though. First crushes, or loves, or obsessions, never really faded away. Right? Jana should know. After all, she was Miss Jewel, the Queen of Dating, at least to the masses out there who didn't even know her real name, or the fact that she lived in a teeny tiny Texan town where the biggest thing during the year was the rodeo.

Yep. Cowboys and cowgirls, roping calves, riding bulls, and racing around barrels.

None of it Jana could do. In fact, she hadn't watched a rodeo since *he* left town.

She couldn't. It only reminded her once again how she'd failed at everything she'd tried. Failed to get into college. Failed to get any of her novels published. Failed to be friends with her older sister. Failed to heal her broken heart. Failed to move on.

Jana had read enough self-help books and written

enough advice columns to know that she was in a rut. Problem was, the rut was so deep and the bottom so muddy that she hadn't been able to get out, no matter how many promising green bushes she tried to grab onto.

Her phone alarm went off, pulling Jana from her thoughts. It was time to get to work—her real job, that is. The one that paid the bills at her parents' small farmhouse. They'd left their business to Jana and her sister, but only Jana had stayed.

Natalie was the brains out of the two sisters and had gone on to college, then law school. She didn't want to live in a tiny town and get her hands dirty—or sticky, as the case would be with the homemade jams that their parents had turned into a fledgling business. One that Mr. and Mrs. Harris had mostly retired from. They spent their time in San Antonio, living at a country club, and golfing or playing tennis every day. Who would have thought?

Not Jana. Her parents weren't ranchers. They didn't have enough property for that, not after her grandpa had sold off parcel after parcel, and never invested a dime. Her mom had come up with the idea of making homemade jams, and her dad had locked down a distributor. Now, Harris Farms Preserves were sold in most small-town grocery stores from here to San Antonio. Not quite large enough to move out of the farmhouse kitchen, but busy enough that Jana spent four to six hours a day on the business.

Her dad still ran the financial side of the business, and her mom managed the website and customer service. It was up to Jana to make the jam, fill the jars, and ensure the pickup went smoothly when the truck came to collect the jam jars.

On today's to-do list was making raspberry jam batches.

But her phone rang before she finished unloading a crate

of new jars. Jana frowned when she answered. "What's up, Barb?" Her friend didn't usually call in the middle of the day.

"You're not gonna believe this, hon," Barb said, her voice a gushing tidal wave. "Not in a million years. Or a hundred million years."

Suffice it to say, Barb could be a bit over-the-top, and she was probably the biggest gossip in Prosper. But Jana had no problem being entertained. "Oh yeah? Are you going to make me guess that long?"

Barb scoffed. "I don't have all day, hon. Besides, it's burning my tongue."

"Then out with it," Jana said with a laugh.

"Mayor Prosper had the lineup for this weekend's rodeo on the computer screen at the arena office," Barb said. "It was there in plain sight, so I didn't think there'd be any harm in looking, you know? Just to see which fine cowboys might be coming to our little town."

Jana opened the cupboard and pulled out a box of pectin she bought in bulk. "I thought this was burning your tongue. Out with it."

Barb took a breezy breath. "Make sure you're not holding one of those pretty jam jars of yours, because I don't want you to drop it."

"Barb . . ."

"Okay, hon." Another breath. "*Knox Prosper* entered the bull-riding. He's coming back to Prosper."

Jana was glad she was alone in her kitchen, and she was glad she wasn't holding a jam jar after all. Barb was still talking—speculating, of course—but Jana hadn't heard anything after the name *Knox Prosper*.

It was him.

The guy she hadn't gotten over. The guy who she'd been in love with ever since she could remember—she and every female within fifty miles of Prosper. The guy who'd dumped her right before prom and hadn't spoken to her since. The guy who'd married another woman in a shotgun wedding. That woman then divorced him, returned to Prosper with their kid, and before anyone knew what time of day it was, married his brother.

Knox Prosper had made himself scarce for a long time. Years, really. He'd come into town only once last year for the rodeo, did the bull-riding then, too. But that was before he'd gotten some fame on the pro-rodeo circuit. Yeah, he was making a name for himself now. Which, of course, made him even more off-limits to Jana. He hadn't ever explained why he'd stopped talking to her, and she doubted he ever would.

Good riddance.

"Thanks for the warning." Jana cut off Barb with a fake, breezy laugh. "Not like I was planning on going, anyway."

"I know, hon," Barb said. "But what kind of friend would I be if I didn't tell you first? You know, before someone else did."

"Right," Jana said. "So are we still on for tomorrow night at Racoons?"

"Sure thing, hon. Girls night out."

"Perfect." Jana turned to gaze out the kitchen window that overlooked the neighbor's ranch. Ten-year-old Ellie McIverson was out riding her horse like usual. That girl never seemed to quit.

After Barb hung up, Jana finally allowed herself to react to the news about Knox coming into town again. Of course he'd come to Prosper. His kid was here. His entire family was here, and word was—from Barb—that he'd made amends. Mostly. How much amends could really be made when your ex-wife had married your brother?

Jana closed her eyes and eased out a long breath.

She was over him. There was no reason for any butterflies to be tickling her skin right now. For all she knew, he had a girlfriend, or two or three. Knox had never lacked in the ladies department.

Which was why he should totally and completely repel her.

She knew better than to let her heart continue to chase after a guy like him. A guy who'd never be faithful. A guy who'd never be hers even if he changed.

Her phone rang again, and Jana sighed. Apparently, she wasn't getting a break today. It was Natalie, which meant this was a business call. Her sister texted when she wanted to be social, emailed when she didn't want Jana to forget something, and called when it was urgent business.

"Hello," Jana answered.

"Jana, you got a few minutes?" Natalie's tone was brusque. Without waiting for a reply, she said, "Mom and Dad are on the phone. Hang on, let me conference everyone together."

One second, then two, then Natalie said, "Jana, you still there?"

"Yep," Jana said. "Still here." No one laughed.

"Hello, dear," her mother said, her tone the typical disconnected breathy quality as always.

"Hi, Mom," Jana said.

"All right," her dad cut in. "Natalie was telling us about a new inventory software one of her clients built. We're going to start implementing it at the end of the month. Right now, I'm taking a training class on it here in San Antonio, then I can teach you, Jana."

"Okay," Jana said, frowning. "Why don't I come and train? Then it will cut that time in half." She knew her dad always appreciated time shortcuts.

"No, you're right where you need to be," her dad continued without any pause. "I don't want to have to cover your end of the production with one of those pimply kids who will break jars."

"Besides," Natalie cut in, "this software company is interested in having Dad sit on their board. So this will be an excellent boon to him."

Jana's dad sat on more than one company's boards, as a consultant for product development. He'd originally started Harris Farms Preserves for her mom specifically because she wanted her own company. The thing had taken off—modestly—and now provided Jana's living. But at times, she felt like the most unsupported employee in Texas.

"That's wonderful, dear," her mother said, now speaking to her dad. "But I thought you were going to cut back. We're supposed to be retired."

Her dad's chuckle was empty. "We could give up the country club membership, if that's what you're asking."

"Of course not," her mother murmured.

Jana exhaled, having heard this exact conversation more times than not.

"It's settled, then," her dad said. "Natalie is adding it to our company bylaws."

"All right," Jana said. It wasn't like she'd have a choice. Once her dad made up his mind, it was made up.

2

"Hi, baby girl." Knox Prosper crouched so that he was eye level with his five-year-old daughter.

Right now, Ruby had her freckled nose scrunched, and her brown eyes, so much like her mom's, narrowed at him.

"You forgot my birf-day."

Heat raced through Knox, but he pushed away the guilt. One of those books he'd read about rekindling broken relationships had counseled to not let the first emotion become too overwhelming. Guilt, embarrassment, regret—they were all there, burning up his chest right now.

"I'm sorry about that, baby." Knox tucked a bit of curly hair behind Ruby's ear. They were outside his parents' home—neutral turf for them both—and Knox was sitting with his daughter on the porch swing. "But there's one good thing about a late birthday wish."

Ruby's eyes rounded. "Like what?"

She was getting too smart for her own good.

"It means you get even more presents." Knox reached for the sack that Ruby had been eying the past few minutes. "How old are you?"

"Five," Ruby said, sounding as if she were personally offended that her own daddy didn't know her age.

Knox held back a chuckle. "Five, huh? Well, looks like I guessed right." He reached into the sack and pulled out a wrapped gift. "Because that's how many presents I got in here."

"Five presents?" Ruby said. "All for me?"

"That's right, baby girl," Knox said. "All for you. And I hope you can forgive me for not calling you last week."

Ruby was grinning, and Knox wondered for the thousandth time how he ever got so lucky to have a daughter like her. She was literally the sun in his life.

"I forgive you, Daddy." Ruby's small arms wrapped around his neck in a chokehold.

Even though he couldn't exactly breathe, he pulled her closer. "Thank you."

"Can I open them now?" Ruby pulled back, her brown eyes as serious as he'd ever seen them.

His mouth quirked. "Yes, right now."

He was pretty sure this was considered bribing his kid, buying her love or whatnot. And he was pretty sure that his ex-wife, Macie, could hear every word of their conversation through the front screen door. Later, she'd also tell about what he'd done wrong, Macie wouldn't fail him in that. It might have bugged him—no, infuriated him—a few months ago. But now . . .

It wasn't like Knox had done a one-eighty in his life. He still had plenty of flaws, and some of them major, but he'd done maybe a one-ten? And he was working on the other seventy degrees of change. Because if there was one thing he did want in life, even more than his aspirations on the pro-rodeo circuit, it was to do right by the little girl sitting next to him.

"A unicorn?" Ruby exclaimed. "I love it, Daddy! Now I have *two* unicorns."

Knox bit back a groan. Of course, he had no idea which toys his daughter did or didn't have. How could he? He'd never been inside of her bedroom at the home she currently lived in with Macie and Holt. And Knox didn't have any immediate plans to change that, either.

Now, he watched Ruby open the second gift.

"Bubbles!" she squealed. "I love bubbles!"

Knox chuckled. His daughter wasted no time in sliding off the porch swing and opening the bubbles. But she'd opened them on an angle, and half the liquid spilled out.

"Whoa, there," Knox said, grasping the bottle and tilting it upright. "Maybe we can do this after you open the other presents."

"It spilled," Ruby said, her small teeth biting down on her lower lip.

"Just a little," Knox soothed. "We can make some more, if you want."

Her forehead wrinkled as her pretty brown eyes studied him. "Do you know how to make bubbles?"

How hard could it be? "Sure do, baby girl."

"Okay." Ruby set the sudsy bottle into his hands.

He felt like he'd been slimed, and he discreetly wiped his hands on his jeans, which had seen much better days.

Ruby tore into the third present, then the fourth, and finally, the fifth.

Perhaps Knox had gone overboard. But there'd been plenty of things he hadn't paid for in his marriage that he should have. And today, he was taking the first step to set that all straight, too. It would still take a while to pay back his brother Holt what he owed, but every bit would help.

Ruby yawned as she clutched her five new toys to her chest. Macie had warned him it was nearly nap time, but Knox hadn't wanted to wait any longer. Later this afternoon, more family would be around, and all he had the strength to deal with right now was his little girl.

"Are you tired, baby girl?" Knox smoothed her hair back, then kissed the top of her head.

Ruby gave a solemn nod. He loved that about her. She was always true to her feelings.

"Let's get you inside, then," he said. "You napping at Grandpa's house?"

Ruby had the entire extended family wrapped around her little fingers, but especially her grandpa, Rex Prosper, who happened to also be the mayor of the city founded by his great-grandad.

Ruby nodded again, and since she was looking so small and her eyes seemed so heavy, he scooped her into his arms and carried her into the house.

Everything about the house was familiar. His mom hadn't changed much in the way of décor over the years. The same afghan was thrown over the back of the couch, the leather recliner sat where it always sat, and in the kitchen, everything was the same, too.

There, Macie sat at the table, with her bracelet-making equipment spread across it. He knew she had plenty of room at his brother's house, but Ruby loved the ranch. Knox guessed that Holt was keeping to the barn during the visit, which was just as well. Although peace had been made between them as far as Macie marrying Holt, it wasn't like they were going to hang out together. Not unless it was necessary.

Macie looked up as he carried Ruby toward the hallway where the bedrooms were.

"You ready for your nap, sweetie?" she asked, rising from the table.

"I've got her," Knox said. "Evie's room, right?"

Macie nodded, her gaze tracking him and cataloging the toys gripped in Ruby's arms.

Knox didn't explain anything but continued walking until he reached his sister Evie's room. She was living in San Antonio now and working for a newspaper. Her boyfriend was there, too, and Knox supposed Carson Hunt was a nice enough kid.

The room was dim since the curtains were half-closed, and Ruby's eyes remained half-open as Knox set her down on the bed. She refused to let go of her toys, and instead, clutched them to her chest as Knox unfolded a blanket, then draped it over her small form.

"Sleep tight, baby girl," he whispered as Ruby's eyelids drifted closed. He pressed a kiss to her temple, then stood for a moment, watching his miracle sleep.

A miracle because she'd been unexpected. That first night Knox had met Macie at the rodeo so many years ago, they'd danced, then gone for a drive in his truck about Prosper. It was her first time in the town, and he was glad for a break from seeing Jana Harris with her friends—laughing and dancing with whoever asked them to dance.

Jana hadn't even cared that he'd come looking for her before the bull-riding. No, when he'd approached where she was sitting with her group, everyone acknowledged him but her. She never once looked up from her phone.

He'd kept silent for long enough, but it was time to finally hear why she'd betrayed him in her own words. He'd let things fester for months. But no more.

But Jana had ignored him. Acted like he didn't exist. Like he wasn't even good enough to wipe her boots on.

So Knox had left her little circle of friends and joined up with his fellow bull-riders. No bull could have thrown him that night, and Knox ended up winning the championship. So, he'd celebrated by dancing with a pretty girl from out of town. Macie had been completely different from Jana. Macie had listened to his stories; her laugh was soft and her smile sweet.

Yeah, things had gone too far, too fast that night. And when Macie told him she was pregnant, there wasn't even a question in Knox's mind. He proposed marriage on the spot to her, and provided a home for his new wife and kid.

Until he didn't. Until he could never seem to get a break. Never get both feet under him. Never have a decent night's sleep. Never stop being bothered by Jana's betrayal. On one level, he knew that Macie was different. That she'd never do such a thing. But what did he know about women, truly know about them?

He'd hit rock bottom, hard, and Macie and Ruby were the ones to pay the dearest price.

By the time he realized what he'd lost and given up, it was too late to turn things around.

Macie had moved on. Completely.

Knox knew it was over, totally, but moments like this . . . watching his baby girl sleeping made him wish he wasn't only stopping in for a few moments. He released a slow breath, then turned to the door. He stepped out into the hall, and closed the door with a soft click.

"She's asleep?" Macie asked quietly.

Knox looked over to see her standing at the end of the hall, arms folded, as she leaned against the wall.

She'd always been beautiful, but it seemed wrong to appreciate it any longer. So much time had passed, so many hurtful words, and even more hurtful feelings . . . She was no longer his to notice such things as her dark hair tumbling over her shoulders, the soft pink of her cheeks . . .

"Yeah," he said. "Ruby went out quick."

Macie's smile was gentle, and Knox pushed away that pang in his chest.

He walked down the hall, nearing her before he paused. "I got her a few presents. I'm sorry again for missing her birthday."

He'd seen the hurt expression on Macie's face plenty of times in the past, but not today. Her face remained relaxed, her gaze understanding. "I'm glad you came today, Knox. Ruby was so excited, and when she wakes up, she'll probably demand to call you."

Knox smiled at this. "She's got my number, sugar." He nearly bit his tongue at the old endearment he used to call Macie.

But she let it slide, thank goodness.

"Well, I should be going," he said. "Lots to prepare for." He moved past her. Macie didn't step away from the wall, but watched him leave.

Once on the porch, he retrieved his cowboy hat from the porch swing.

He strode down the driveway to where he'd parked his beat-up truck in the shade. Was Macie watching him leave? Was Holt, from wherever he was in the barn?

If only Knox had kept his head screwed on straight that night he'd met Macie. She'd been talking to Holt first, but when Knox approached, he was seething at Jana's rejection. Once again. So he'd asked Macie to the dirt dance, if only to show Jana that he wasn't sitting around waiting for an apology.

And now, his entire life had become one apology after another.

3

THERE WAS NO reason to think that Knox Prosper would be at Racoons tonight, so why Jana was taking twice as long to get ready, she didn't know. Her dark red hair was less curly than it had been when she was a kid. She'd spent time every day during her teen years straightening her hair. But now, she'd embraced the curly again. Fortunately, she didn't have to deal with frizz, but rather coaxed the waves into submission.

She touched up her makeup, which was already perfect, but it was her shield between everyone out there and her heart. Another layer of plum lipstick went on, then she stepped back from the mirror to survey the rest of her. Her dress was a navy print wrap-around, and she decided on the heeled sandals that weren't her favorite to dance in, but she loved them nonetheless.

A horn honked outside, undoubtedly Barb.

Yep. Sure enough, a text chimed in a second later. *We're here.*

Jana turned off the lights as she left the house, then locked the door. Not that the town of Prosper was crime ridden, but fresh homemade jam might be a draw for some.

Jana climbed into the back seat of Barb's Cadillac since Patsy was in the front seat already.

"You're smokin' hot, Jana," Barb said with a laugh. Her platinum blonde hair fell about her shoulders like a waterfall, and her silver dress hugged every toned curve. Barb was perfection in itself. "Anyone special coming tonight?"

Jana fought back a blush. "Not that I know of."

"Ohhh, did you hear?" Patsy said, twisting in her seat as Barb started driving. Patsy's short dark hair was spiked up on one side, and her dark, cat-like eyes were rounded with anticipation. "Knox Prosper is in town. I saw him at the gas station today."

Barb's gaze met Jana's in the rearview mirror. Barb winked, and Jana rolled her eyes.

"I appreciate all the updates on Knox, but really, I don't care," Jana said in perhaps too sharp of a tone. "We were over a long time ago."

"I know, babe, but he's *single* again."

"Mm-hmm," Barb said, her smile a grin.

"I don't want another woman's leftovers," Jana said.

"Oooo!" Patsy squealed. "Someone is feisty tonight."

Barb laughed and turned up the music, a welcome reprieve from talking about Knox Prosper. If he did show up at Racoons tonight, then he'd be the last person she'd talk to.

The place was packed. New blood in town from all the cowboys arriving for the rodeo, which meant all the ladies had shown up in full force. Jana headed to the bar with her friends, and while they waited for their drinks, she checked out the place. The dance floor was hopping, and most of the tables were full of groups of men and women chatting and flirting.

Everyone was checking everyone else out, and for some reason, Jana was annoyed. It wasn't any surprise, of course, since it was par for the course with a bar scene. But Jana hated that she'd gotten her hopes up. Knox Prosper wasn't here, and that shouldn't matter one way or another to her. Yet, it did.

"I'm going outside for a bit," Jana told Barb.

"What? Why?"

"Have a headache coming on." And it was true. Jana weaved her way through the patrons, only to be stopped twice and asked for a dance. She turned both cowboys down and continued outside. Others had congregated outside, talking and joking loudly in their groups, but Jana bypassed them all.

She headed into the back parking lot, which was filled, and leaned against someone's truck as she gazed up at the summer night sky.

The stars twinkled down at her as if oblivious to the turmoil her heart and mind were going through.

She couldn't live like this anymore. Couldn't look around every corner for Knox when she knew he was in town. Couldn't keep comparing the men she dated to what she and Knox used to have. It had been a long time since there'd been anything between them, and everything she'd heard about him since should have sent her running.

Yet, here she was, by herself at the back of Racoons. Avoiding, once again.

There were plenty of men inside, ones who might be a great match for her. Yet, she'd turned down their invitations to dance. Why? Because she wanted to sit in a corner and wait for Knox to show up? What if he did? What would she do?

Nothing, that's what. At least, that's what she'd always done. Whenever he came around, she pointedly ignored him. Just like that night at the rodeo years ago—the night he'd apparently met Macie. Everyone knew it was a shotgun wedding, but that didn't mean Jana hadn't felt hurt that Knox had pledged himself to another woman. Which was ridiculous, since they'd been broken up for months.

Why?

That was the question that had haunted her for years.

And she was sick of it. She wanted answers, no matter how awkward or uncomfortable the conversation. She wanted to know, once and for all, why Knox Prosper had so thoroughly ghosted her.

Until that night at the rodeo . . . She knew he'd wanted to talk to her. But she'd panicked, shut down, and instead of looking up at him and greeting him, giving him an inch, she'd not looked at him once. At least not until he'd walked away.

Jana pulled out her phone and texted Barb. *Not feeling so great. Can you take me home really quick?*

Barb replied, *Ah, sorry. I'll be out soon.*

Jana couldn't explain the relief she felt on the drive back to her place. Even if Knox did show up at Racoons, it wasn't really the ideal place to get her answers. She'd figure out a different way, even if she had to go so far as to get his number from his mom.

"Are you sure you're gonna be okay, hon?" Barb asked as she pulled up in front of Jana's house.

"I just need to go to bed early," she said. "Always the magic cure for a headache."

Barb's made-up face looked almost comically sad. "Is this about Knox not showing up tonight? You know the night is still young."

"No, it's nothing like that," Jana said quickly. She opened her door. "Thanks again, and sorry for being a party pooper."

"Feel better," Barb said. "But know that you owe me one."

Jana smiled, then shut the door and headed to the dark house. She didn't flip on lights as she made her way to the bathroom to undo what she'd done up just an hour earlier. Why she'd even bothered sometimes, she didn't know.

Her phone chimed with an incoming email to her column. She touched her phone screen and read the message.

Not Over You

Dear Miss Jewel,
I'm hung up on my high school boyfriend still. It's been two years, and we've both moved on. But I keep checking his social media. Help?
Brynn, lost in Austin

"You and me, both, honey," Jana murmured to herself. Her advice should be to stop following the guy's social media. To avoid places that reminded her of her ex. To find a new hobby to keep her busy . . .

All things that Jana had done. All things that hadn't worked. Because here she was, her heart tied up in knots, just knowing that Knox Prosper was in the same town. He could be out there, anywhere.

Jana would answer in the morning. Then she'd get back to the novel she'd been working on. And she'd finish the raspberry jam batch. She'd do all the things. But tonight, she'd crash and sleep.

Yet, sleep didn't come for a long time, and then when it finally did, her alarm went off only a few hours later. She tried to go back to sleep for another hour, but her mind started to turn over the events of last night. Which were quite uneventful. Lost hopes, really.

So, she dragged herself out of bed. Showered and changed into a red T-shirt and ratty jeans. Nothing that would be ruined by raspberries or pectin. Texts had come in from Barb and Patsy late last night, telling her that Knox had never showed. Whatever. She didn't care about that. She'd find a way to track him down on her own. Without a crowd at a bar as witnesses.

But for now, she had to finish two dozen more jars. Pickup would be later this afternoon, and she needed the jam completely processed and cooled by then. She began to set out the jars, only to find she was four jars short. She recounted, then double-checked the boxes of jars that she'd picked up a few days ago. One of the boxes must have been short.

Jana sighed. This would put her back about thirty minutes, since she'd now have to run to the grocery store and get four jars. She took off her apron, hung it over a kitchen chair, then tugged on a pair of old cowboy boots. Not bothering to spruce up her appearance, she headed to the small SUV that needed a new paint job and probably new tires.

Oh, and a CD player would be nice. But she cranked the radio anyway, rolled down the windows, and drove off the property. The summer morning was beautiful, and Jana would never complain about the wide blue Texan sky or the stillness of the countryside. A small town had its advantages—everyone knew each other, and everyone helped each other. Which was why she slowed down when she saw a truck pulled over on the side of the road at an odd angle. That, and the hood was open. Obviously, the truck had broken down, and she caught a glimpse of a man checking out something beneath the hood.

He probably knew what he was doing, but the walk into town was a ways, so if he needed an auto part . . .

Jana braked, then stopped. She backed up until she was closer to the truck. By then, the guy had turned around. The second Jana realized who it was, she wished she would have kept driving.

Knox Prosper stood there, his shirt off, his jeans slung low, his cowboy hat perched atop his head. In one hand, he held a dirty rag, and the other rested on his hip as he watched her backing up. No, she was pretty sure he didn't recognize her yet. It wasn't like she had this little SUV in high school.

She might have wanted to get the truth out of Knox Prosper, but not this way. Apparently, the joke was on her.

4

KNOX HAD KNOWN his truck was surviving on a prayer to even make it as far as his hometown. But he'd brought it regardless, needing to haul his rodeo stuff. He didn't trust it on a plane—besides, he wasn't flying back to Montana. He was done with that place, and he'd already been picked up by the pro circuit in Texas.

What he hadn't wanted to happen was this exact scenario. Stranded on the roadside just when his time slot for practicing at the rodeo grounds was about to start.

Maybe the cowboy who'd pulled over on the side of the road could take him into town really quick to get a U-joint—at least, he hoped that was what needed to be fixed. But no cowboy climbed out of the older model SUV. A least not of the male variety. And he couldn't have been more surprised if five clowns had popped out of the vehicle when he saw that the person now walking toward him was none other than Jana Harris.

It was like he'd wished her here. Well, not *here*, exactly, but into a place where he could finally talk to her. Yet, the timing couldn't be worse.

Jana was no longer the teenager he remembered—her curves and the sharper definition of her face were that of a grown woman. She wore sunglasses atop her hair, and yeah, he remembered all that red hair. Except it was darker now, almost an auburn. She wore a red T-shirt, black cowboy boots, and body-hugging jeans that would probably cause a car wreck in a bigger city.

But Knox wasn't checking her out. Nope. Not at all. Because Jana Harris was one hundred percent off-limits—maybe even two hundred percent. Some things just couldn't be forgiven.

Still, his gaze flicked to her left hand, but he didn't see a wedding ring. Not that it would matter. At least not to him. And there was no sign of her smile—the one that used to make him rewrite every single one of his dreams about leaving Prosper and becoming a rodeo star. That had eventually happened, but in the most backward way possible.

Jana didn't look happy; in fact, she looked mad.

So, why had she stopped in the first place?

"Jana," he said, the word almost foreign to his tongue. He might have thought about her a few dozen—or a few hundred—times, but it had been years since he'd actually spoken her name. "Uh, thanks for stopping. I'm kind of in a bind here." He motioned toward the open hood of his truck, as if it weren't obvious.

Jana stopped a few feet from him, and he could swear he smelled raspberries. Folding her arms, her gaze slid past him to the engine of the truck.

Yep. She still had those dusky hazel eyes. And those freckles that he'd tried to count one time.

"What seems to be the problem?"

Knox rubbed at the perspiration forming on the back of his neck. Had he been sweating before she pulled over? She wasn't looking at him, but that didn't seem to matter. It was still early in the morning, but it felt as if the noonday sun was beating upon him. "I don't exactly know, but I'm hoping it's a U-joint."

Jana's hazel eyes shifted to him once again. Her gaze flickered down, then up.

Was *she* checking *him* out?

"You need a ride into town to get that part?" she asked, her arms folded, her jawline tight. But no matter how tense she acted, her lips still looked soft.

Knox blinked. "That would be great, ma'am. Unless you're in a hurry. I can wait for the next person to come along."

Jana's brows lifted. "The only other person who might come along this morning is Bud McIverson, and he's gone before the roosters crow." She turned then and began walking toward her SUV. "If you're coming with me, put a shirt on."

Knox stared after her, then he felt laughter bubble in his chest. The shirt was no problem. Not at all. He dropped the hood of his truck, then reached into the open driver's side window and snatched the button-down he'd discarded in favor of keeping it semi-clean while he checked out his truck's engine. It wasn't like he was staying in a fancy hotel with a laundry room.

The SUV was already running when he climbed into the passenger seat. Sitting this close to Jana confirmed what he'd smelled. "Been picking raspberries?"

Jana didn't answer for a moment as she pulled on the road.

In fact, as the silence stretched between them, Knox wondered if he should just drop the small talk and come right out with his question.

But then, she said, "I'm making raspberry jam."

Knox looked over at her, surprised. "That's very domestic of you." He used to tease her about not ever having any desire to cook or bake.

Her gaze didn't move from the road ahead of them. "It's a business. My parents. They live in San Antonio now, and I fill the orders."

Knox hadn't expected any of this. Jana had been the kind of girl who was always reading a book in high school. So much so, it had affected her grades, or at least that's what her parents had accused her of. If he remembered right, her older sister had been valedictorian or something.

"Huh, that's great," he said. "Do you like it? I never thought you'd be a baker—or whatever it's called. A jam-maker?"

She looked at him then, and her hazel eyes were cool. Almost frosty.

"Whoa," he said. "What did I say wrong?"

"Sometimes, people do things because it's the right thing to do," she said. "Not because they *want* to. Never mind, you wouldn't understand."

Knox frowned. "What do you mean by that?"

Jana stepped on the brake, and instead of answering his question, she said, "Here's your stop."

Knox looked out his window. They were at the mechanic shop. "Thanks for the ride and all. But can you tell me why you don't think I'd understand?"

Jana seemed to be debating something, then she looked at him again. This time, the frostiness was gone, only to be replaced by something else . . . hurt?

"You always did what you wanted, Knox," she said. "I mean, everyone thought you were cool for not caring what others hoped for you. I guess I was one who fell for your charm and your don't-give-a-crap attitude. You made everything look so easy, so fun and entertaining. But after high school, the real world kicked in. For me, at least. Not for you, obviously."

Knox narrowed his eyes. "That's pretty harsh coming from someone who made her own decisions without thinking of anyone but herself."

Jana put the SUV into park, although the engine was still idling. "What are you even talking about?"

"I'm talking about you getting pregnant and not telling me."

Jana's mouth opened. Then closed. A red stain creeped up her neck.

Knox felt sick all over again. He'd felt sick when Aaron told him about Jana getting rid of her baby—a baby that could only be his. And he was pretty sure that played into his determination to marry Macie when *she* became pregnant. Not that he wanted to think about any of that now. This had been a mistake. He shouldn't have brought up the past. He couldn't change it, anyway. And the hurt and pain in Jana's eyes only mirrored that in his gut.

Knox reached for the door handle. "Sorry for bothering you." But before he opened the door, Jana grasped his arm.

"Who told you I was pregnant?" she said, her voice shaky.

Knox didn't even want to look at her right now. "It doesn't matter now."

"Knox, tell me," she said, her voice stronger, sharper now. "Who *told* you?"

It was a long time ago, yeah, but he'd never forget. "Aaron Bushnell."

Jana released his arm. "Wow . . . I can't believe—"

"Your little secret got out?" Knox cut in. "You know this is a small town, for better or for worse. It doesn't matter who told me. That has nothing to do with it." Now, he was just plain angry again, and he faced her, not caring that she looked pale beneath the reddening of her face. "But it makes me sick that you wouldn't tell me. Didn't even give me a choice. Yet, you went ahead and got rid of the baby, anyway."

Jana blinked. "What?"

"I'm done here." Knox reached for the door and bailed out of the SUV.

"Knox!" she called after him, climbing out of the SUV.

He stopped, but didn't turn around.

"I was never pregnant," she said, her voice quiet, pained. "It was a false alarm. Aaron must have overheard me say something to Barb or Patsy. His locker was right next to ours."

Knox's heart felt like it had been taken out of his chest and stomped on. He didn't know if it was still beating or not. How was this possible? For years, he'd lived with so much animosity against Jana, only to find out . . .

He spun around. "It wasn't just Aaron who told me, it was—"

"Briggs?"

Knox exhaled. "Yeah."

Jana wiped at tears on her cheeks. "Figures. And it figures you'd believe those idiots. You could have asked *me*, you know. Called me up on the phone. Come over to my house."

"I tried to talk to you," Knox said. "More than once."

"When?" Jana said, but didn't wait for him to answer. "But what should I expect? You're Knox Prosper. God of the high school, with every girl chasing after you. When you told me you liked me, really liked me, I believed you. And that was *my* mistake."

She turned and climbed back into the SUV. Before Knox could fully process their conversation and the horrible revelation of how gossip had twisted both of their lives, she'd driven off. And he was pretty sure she wasn't coming back.

5

JANA PARKED BEHIND the grocery store and rested her forehead on the steering wheel. She couldn't very well walk into the grocery store with her face streaked with tears. At least she hadn't been wearing makeup. After all these years, and all this time, Knox had believed such a huge lie about her. It was so ridiculous that it was laughable, but since it was happening to her, there was nothing to laugh about.

She remembered the day she'd bought the pregnancy test. She'd gone to the next town because she was too mortified to get it in Prosper. When it came back negative, she'd sobbed out her relief, then determined that the one-time interlude with Knox would be her last. She didn't want to be a knocked-up teenager, and there was no way she'd go to any doctor who might know her parents to ask for birth control. Besides, she was pretty sure Knox wasn't the father type.

She'd been more right than she could have ever known then. According to Barb, he was hardly a part of his daughter's life, and he'd been a terrible husband to Macie. It seemed that Jana had lucked out after all.

If so, then why did she feel so terrible now? Yeah, it was tough to think that Knox believed a lie all these years, but really, it was probably a good thing. If they'd talked back in high school, and he'd found out the truth, they probably would have kept dating. And Jana would be the one with an ex-husband now.

She took a deep breath, then released it. Yes, she was lucky. She'd dodged a bullet, as they said. There was nothing to cry about. She could let the pain go now. Knox had answered her question, and now that she knew what had happened to make him break up with her, she could move on.

No longer shackled to a wall of unanswered questions, life could only get better. Right?

Jana checked her appearance in the mirror. Not great, but not terrible, either. She pulled out the spare foundation powder she kept in her purse and smoothed some on. There. Her crying was hardly noticeable now. She'd be in and out of the store in a jiffy, and besides, her car was the only one here this early in the morning.

Ten minutes later, Jana was back in her SUV, having only encountered Trista, the teenage cashier who was putting in summer hours. So far, so good. Jana pulled onto Main Street, drove through town, then turned onto the road that would take her back home. She wasn't all that delayed after all. Making the pickup time wouldn't be a big deal, and she wouldn't have to call and put them off.

She instinctively put her foot on the brake when she saw a man walking up ahead. This time, Jana wasn't fooled. She knew exactly who it was. It seemed that Knox had gotten his truck part, judging by the sack that he carried. Because she'd been the one to pick him up, she knew he still had a way to go before he reached his truck. And he could walk. It was good exercise, right?

She continued driving past him, and he glanced over as she did so. When he lifted his hand in a wave—a wave goodbye, of course—something in Jana's chest jolted. He'd been hurt, too. Despite all the ill thoughts she'd had of him for a very long time, he'd gone through similar emotions. He thought she'd gone behind his back and done something serious without bothering to consult or tell him.

Before Jana knew it, she'd pressed on the brakes and stopped. She closed her eyes and breathed out. Why was she extending the olive branch? She'd have to analyze it later, but for now, she was going with her gut.

She rolled down the passenger side window as Knox approached. She tried not to notice the definition of his tanned forearms as he rested them on the window.

"Must be my lucky day," he said, his green eyes locked on hers.

The softness of his tone cut through her misgivings about stopping. He was grateful, that was clear.

"Get in before I change my mind," she said.

"Yes, ma'am." Knox popped open the door; a second later, he was sitting next to her, making the interior of the SUV seem extremely small.

His long legs barely fit in the space, and his shoulders were broad enough to nearly touch hers. But she wasn't checking him out or noticing his scent of sage and the outdoors. If there was one thing that hadn't changed about Knox Prosper, it was that he never put on airs. He didn't wear cologne, didn't wear fancy shirts, didn't wear any sort of jewelry. He didn't need it. And the whiskers on his chin added another dimension. His raw masculinity was appealing enough.

Stop, Jana.

She started driving, hating how her stomach was all fluttery. "Got what you needed?" she said, not because she necessarily wanted to have a conversation with him, but because she had to say something to keep her thoughts from straying where they shouldn't.

"I hope so," Knox said, opening his sack. He pulled out a U-joint. "Bill seemed to think this will fix it."

Jana nodded. His truck was in sight, just up ahead. "And you know how to put it in?"

Knox chuckled, and despite any walls Jana had put up, the sound made her all melty. "Between Bill's crash course explanation and YouTube, I'm counting on it. I've already had to forfeit my practice time at the arena this morning, so now I have plenty of time."

Jana glanced over at him as she slowed down behind his truck. "Can you do it later today?"

"Nope." Knox set the U-joint back into the sack and reached for the door handle. "I'll just have to go tomorrow." He popped open the door. "Thanks for this. I appreciate the ride, both ways. And I'm sorry about . . . earlier. For all of it. For not finding out for myself and believing two guys I knew were yahoos to begin with."

Jana's throat had gone tight. "I'm sorry, too," she whispered.

Their gazes held. His green eyes were filled with sincerity, regret, sorrow . . . things she'd never expected to see from him. Not in her wildest hopes.

Knox touched the brim of his hat and climbed out. He shut the door, then strode to his truck. Jana didn't move. She didn't pull away. She merely watched him as he popped the hood of his truck and set to work.

"Here I go," she muttered, then climbed out of the car. "Hey, Knox. If that can wait, you can use my car to get to the arena. Just drop me off at home. I'm making jam all morning, so I won't need it."

He turned slowly, his gaze finding hers where she stood like a nervous schoolgirl giving out her first valentine.

"Ah, that's sweet of you to offer, Jana," he said. "But I don't want to impose. I think we both know you'd like to roast me to a blackened crisp over a fire."

Jana blinked, then she felt a smile grow. A very traitorous smile. "You wouldn't be wrong there, Knox. But I can put my agenda off for another day."

His lips quirked, then he grinned. "Well, I'll be." He turned and shut the hood, then he headed her way.

Jana allowed herself a few stolen seconds to admire the cowboy striding toward her. No matter the years and heartache that had passed, Knox Prosper was a beautiful man. On the outside, of course, and something else was peeking through as well. A softer side of him. One that she'd seen in high school when it was just the two of them. He'd always been cocky around everyone else. Perhaps a person could change. Life had a way of knocking you down until you did change.

But right now, with his easy stride, his long legs in those well-worn jeans, the shirt not doing much to hide his sculpted torso created by years of hard rodeo work, the strong line of his jaw, and the quirk of those lips she'd once known so well... *Refocus, Jana. Show's over.*

She slid back into her seat, and when Knox was settled next to her, she drove the rest of the way to her house. Once she parked, she couldn't get out of the SUV fast enough. Before Knox could say anything, she grabbed the jars from the back seat and said, "You know where to find me. Good luck with everything."

Then she hurried toward the house, feeling Knox's gaze on her.

"Thanks again," he called after her.

But she didn't turn around. She only waved, then walked

into the house and shut the door. Leaning against the door, she kept her eyes closed and her body still until she heard him drive away.

Jana opened her eyes, went into the kitchen, and put down her purchases. She needed to focus on the rest of her day and not think about what it was like to be in Knox Prosper's presence again. It was like they'd come to an understanding. Both of them had made mistakes that caused years of painful misunderstanding, and now . . . they could each move on. Separately. Knox would be gone in a few days—off to whichever rodeo event was next—and Jana would still be in Prosper, making jam, and saving relationships one column at a time.

It was fine. And now, she could officially move on. Start dating again. Maybe she'd even go to Racoons tonight and live it up a little. Dance and have fun.

As she worked on the next batch of jam, her mind kept tugging to her laptop, where her unfinished novel sat. It was her third one. The first two had been rejected by multiple publishers, and although she knew she could self-publish it in today's market, if a publisher didn't want it, would any readers?

Once the current batch was cooling, she washed her hands, then sat on the faded floral couch in the living room with her laptop. She reviewed the previous chapter written, and soon, she was typing away. The words seemed to flow, and so what if she was channeling Knox a little bit? She needed real-life examples as a springboard, right?

Somehow, she lost any sense of time, so when a knock came at her door, she was startled from her story. She set her laptop aside and rose to her feet. By the time she opened the door, she'd collected her thoughts and returned to the real world as opposed to the story world.

Not Over You

She knew it was going to be Knox, but for some reason, she still drew in a short breath when she saw him standing on her porch. It was a sight she'd never thought would happen. Ever. Yet, here he was.

His open collar revealed a damp chest, and his jeans were dirt-stained now.

"Brought your SUV back," he said, taking off his hat. His hair was a darker blonde than it had been in high school, and it complemented his golden tan.

"Great, how did it go?"

Knox scrubbed a hand through his hair, which looked damp from his hard work.

Jana swallowed and tried to focus on his eyes, which didn't help settle the awakening butterflies in her stomach.

"Good enough," he said. "It was nice to get a feel for the arena and to check out the bulls that they brought in. There are some powerful ones in the group."

"As there should be, right?"

"Yes, ma'am. We gotta get a feel for what we'll be faced with at the event."

"A *feel*... what do you mean?"

"Well, there's some intangibles in bull-riding," he said in a slow voice. "Feel and effort. Yeah, everyone has to learn to go forward on the jump—you know, when the bull jumps, you can't just sit back or you'll fall off."

Jana nodded. She was following so far.

"And timing and balance are important, but they can be learned—trained, really," he continued. "But the feel and effort can't be taught. You've gotta have instincts. You have to be able to feel how that bull's going to leave the chute. If the bull's going to the right or the left, or if he's going to try to whip you to the outside."

"That's a lot of intuition."

"Sure is." His smile inched out as his gaze trailed the length of her.

Heat zinged through her. *Oh boy.* Knox's lazy gaze had made women turn to Jell-O around him, and it seemed as if that hadn't changed one bit.

He must have realized at the same time how she felt about him standing on her porch, because he cleared his throat and put his hat back on. Then he reached into his back pocket and pulled out a battered wallet. "Let me pay you for the gas and time."

"No, it's okay," Jana said quickly. The last thing she wanted was a sweaty twenty bucks from Knox. It would only make her feel indebted to *him*. She leaned back into the house to check the clock. The pickup should be coming soon.

"Uh, if you can just hang here for a few minutes," she began. "I need to be here for the delivery truck. Then I can take you back to your truck."

"No problem," Knox said, looking about the porch. He moved toward the wooden rocking chair that was somehow still all in one piece.

"You can come inside," Jana said, hiding a sigh. Was she really inviting him in? "You look like you could use some ice water, and a stint of staying out of the sun."

His gaze cut to hers, appreciative yet wary.

She stepped aside, holding open the door. "Come on. I won't bite."

"I'm filthy."

Both of them looked at his jeans.

"You're fine," she said. "Just keep to the kitchen."

The edge of his mouth lifted. "All right, then. Thank you, ma'am."

"You don't need to call me *ma'am*," Jana said as he stepped past her and walked into the house.

Having Knox in the small ranch house made him seem larger than life. Well, technically, he was to her—or *had* been to her. No longer. Even when they were on their short dating stint, she didn't remember him ever coming inside her parents' home.

She saw him eye the open laptop.

"Working two jobs?" he asked.

Why did he have to be so observant? And why did he have to ask questions she didn't want to answer?

"Something like that." She moved to the couch and closed the laptop.

Knox walked into the sunny kitchen and stopped near the table. Whistling low, he said, "You weren't kidding when you said you were making jam."

Jana skirted around him so that she was on the opposite side of the table from him. Which was a good thing in her book. "Yeah. Like I said, it's my parents' business. We send jam to stores all over the county."

Knox picked up a jar of the scarlet red jam. He turned it over, read the label, then looked at her. "Harris Farms Preserves. I like it."

Jana shouldn't have felt pleased at his compliment, but she did. It wasn't like she'd chosen the name or anything. Still . . . She looked away from his penetrating green gaze, because she was suddenly feeling self-conscious. Yeah, she might have changed into a blouse and put on a bit of makeup, knowing that he'd be coming back.

Where was that delivery truck? Jana glanced at the clock on the kitchen wall. Five minutes. She could do this. *Get him a drink, that will take some time.* She turned to the fridge and pulled out a pitcher she kept water in so it would always be cold. Then she opened the freezer and took out the ice-cube tray. They didn't have one of those fridges with ice makers, but she didn't mind.

Knox moved about the kitchen, checking out the makings of jam that she had yet to clean up from this morning. She filled a yellow glass with ice, then added the cold water.

"So, does your sister help out with the business, too?" Knox asked, taking the glass from her, then leaning against the sink. "Natalie, right?"

"Right." Jana poured her own glass of cold water, but forewent the ice. "She left right after high school for college, then went on to law school."

Knox's brows raised. "Wow. That's impressive."

"Yeah." Jana took a long swallow of her water. Knox was watching her, and she didn't know what to make of it. "Our conversations are mostly about business since she's part of the company—at least the legal side. Well, she and my dad put together the operations, and my mom and I just do what we're told. My dad started the jam business as a pet project to keep my mom busy, and it ended up being successful. But now, with their semi-retirement, the production side is up to me."

"You've done an impressive job, too," Knox said.

"What? Making jam? A ten-year-old can do this." Jana hadn't meant to sound bitter, but really, no one could compare a law degree to making jam.

Knox didn't seem to mind her retort. He set his glass down, now empty save for the ice, and moved to the table again. Picking up a jar, he said, "I know a lot of ten-year-olds, and none of them could have done this."

He peeked at her, and she was pretty sure he was about to laugh, although his expression was skillfully schooled.

"Oh, really?" Jana challenged. "You know a lot of ten-year-olds? How many exactly do you know, Mr. Prosper?"

Knox looked up at the ceiling, as if he had to count them

all in his mind. When their gazes connected again, he said, "Okay, so maybe I don't know any ten-year-olds personally, but I am a grown man, and I couldn't do any of this."

Jana set her glass down, then rested her hands on her hips. "Sure, you could. It's easy, once you learn in the first place."

Knox set the jar down and tilted his head while studying Jana.

She wouldn't blush—nope, she wouldn't. She was *way* past any connection with Knox Prosper, and all her feelings were in the past.

"My mom would probably faint on the spot if she heard me say this," Knox said in a slow voice, "but I'd love to learn to make jam."

Jana felt like fainting on the spot herself. As it was, she placed one hand on the counter behind her. "You would, huh? And why's that?"

Knox picked up another jam jar and acted like he was studying it, but Jana wasn't fooled. He was stalling to come up with an answer. "Seems like a good and useful skill to have. I mean, I can't ride bulls forever."

The laughter burst out of Jana, completely unexpected. She covered her mouth to stop any more outbursts.

Knox smiled as he set down the jar and folded his arms. "What? You don't think this old cowboy can learn new tricks?"

Jana had to stop grinning. This was ridiculous. She couldn't fall into any sort of friendly pattern with Knox. "I just don't get *why* you want to learn. You don't seem much the homemaker type."

"Are you being sexist, ma'am?" Knox said, his face straight.

Jana laughed. "Not at all . . . I'm being Knox-ist, I guess."

He dipped his chin. "Fair enough. But I'm serious, Jana. I'd like to learn if you're willing to teach me."

Her pulse fluttered, and instead of giving into wanting to tell him yes, she said, "How about I think about it, cowboy?"

6

HAD KNOX EVER worked so hard to get a woman's number? Not in his recollection. But telling Jana he was truly interested in learning the art of jam-making had led to the segue of asking for her number.

"So we can agree on a time," he told her in the kitchen that looked like it contained every raspberry in the state of Texas.

Jana was good about staying on the opposite side of the table from him, which was a smart thing to do. Because if there was one thing Knox was realizing, it was that Jana was even more beautiful than he remembered. Her beauty was only one part of her, though; it was her character that he'd been most drawn to in high school.

Okay, so he wasn't crushing on her. Not at all. He was just analyzing another person's character, like one did from time to time. Jana had caught his attention in high school when they were in English class together. Yeah, he'd always known who the curvy redhead Jana Harris was. But their senior year, something had changed over the summer, and the girl who sat two rows in front of him had gone from sweet hometown girl to stunning.

She'd been standoffish toward him at first, and he

couldn't really blame her since he did have a bit of a reputation. She had her friends; he had his. That had also complicated things, because he'd dated two of her friends, albeit briefly.

Now, Jana was reaching into the back pocket of her jeans. Ones that he liked very much. She pulled out her phone and said, "What's your number?"

It was a good thing to hear. He recited his number, and she sent a text to it.

Just then, a truck pulled up outside the house. "They're here," Jana said in a rush, "and I forgot to load the jars into their boxes."

Knox jumped in to help, wondering about the blush staining her cheeks. They loaded the boxes quickly, and by the time the delivery guy was ready for the last one, the box was loaded.

"Thanks," Jana told the delivery guy, and gave him a tip.

Knox watched her as she interacted with the delivery guy—Jed something or other. Jed certainly wasn't immune to her charms, and Knox wondered if Jana had a boyfriend.

Would it be too forward to ask? There was a time he wouldn't have even thought twice about asking a woman if she was in a relationship, but he was the new Knox. Or at least, he was trying to be.

Jana turned to him next. "Ready to get back to your broken truck?" she said, her tone light, which was a definite improvement from when she'd first stopped and talked to him.

"Yep," he said.

"Okay, great," she said. "I'll just grab my keys."

He probably shouldn't have stared after her as she walked into the house. He was just curious, that was all. Here in Prosper, he should be focusing on only two things. Winning the bull-riding and spending some time with his daughter. Which he'd do tonight. And he'd already done his rodeo practice. So that left fixing his truck and wishing that Jana wasn't going to be dropping him off soon.

Jana came out of the house again, keys in her hand. He wasn't positive, but it looked like she'd put on some lip gloss. Had her lips been shiny earlier? Should he be noticing? They headed to her SUV, and after they both climbed in, Knox said, "If you're not too busy, I'm happy to treat you to lunch. You know, as a thank you."

Jana looked over at him with raised eyebrows as she started the engine. "I don't think that's a good idea. I still haven't decided on the jam thing, and lunch in public would feel . . . a bit much."

"You're probably right." He rolled down the window and let in the warm breeze as they drove. From his peripheral vision, he could see that Jana was smiling, though.

"I'm sure there are plenty of other women in Prosper who'd jump at the chance," she continued. "You know, hanging out with the town rodeo legend, and all."

Knox slapped a hand on his chest. "You're wounding me."

Jana laughed, and he grinned. "Save it for someone else, cowboy. I'm not one of your rodeo chicks."

Knox groaned and pulled his hat down over his eyes. "You did not just say that." He felt the SUV slow.

"We're here," Jana said.

He lifted his hat to see that she'd pulled over next to his truck, but he wasn't done with their conversation. "This is your last chance. Lunch?"

She shook her head. "I've got a busy day, and no offense, but running out of jars, then helping you out this morning put me behind schedule."

"More jam-making?" he said. "I can help with that."

"No, I have other deadlines," she said.

"Like what?"

Her cheeks flushed, and she looked away.

"A second job, or something?" Knox pressed. "With that laptop?" He didn't know why he was so curious, but he was.

"I write a column," she said, glancing at him, then away. "So I really should get back to it. Good luck with everything, Knox."

"Whoa," he said. "Are you about to tell me to have a nice life?"

Her hands were gripping the steering wheel so tight, her knuckles were turning white. He rested a hand atop hers. She flinched, and he pulled away.

"I think that's amazing," he said. "You're a writer. I'm not surprised. I don't think I would have passed English if it weren't for you."

Now, her cheeks were definitely pink, and then he remembered. Most of their study sessions had turned into kissing sessions.

"Well," she said, smoothing her hair behind her ear, "thanks."

"You coming to the rodeo tomorrow?" he asked, thinking it was a pretty standard question, but her eyes darted to him, then away.

"I don't think so."

"Why not?"

She shrugged, and he wished he could see what was going on in that pretty head of hers. "I've really got to go."

Knox could take a hint, or three. He popped open the door and climbed out, but before leaving, he leaned back in and said, "When you make up your mind about the jam, call me. You got my number."

She bit her lip. "Okay."

"I can be to your place in five minutes," he teased.

She didn't laugh, though. "Where you staying? Prosperity Ranch?"

They both knew it was on the other side of town, hardly five minutes away. "Uh, no. Not quite ready for that much family bonding. Things are . . . complicated in that neck of the woods."

He didn't blame her for the curious look she gave him.

"So you're staying at the bed and breakfast? You're lucky you got a room there."

"Not exactly," he said. "It was booked, and so was everything else within miles around."

A line appeared between her brows, then her eyes widened. "Don't tell me you're sleeping in your truck?"

"You caught me," he said nonchalantly. "Keeps me humble. Now, have a good rest of your day, ma'am, and don't delete my number."

Jana only stared at him, and he couldn't guess what was going through her mind. He straightened then shut the door, heading to his truck. He sure hoped that the new U-joint would do the trick. The last thing he needed right now was a major truck repair.

He didn't look up when Jana's SUV turned around in the road and headed back the way they'd come. But his thoughts stayed with her. He wondered what might have happened between them if he had confronted her all those years ago in high school about the rumors he'd been told. Would they have stayed together? Would he have ever asked Macie to the dirt dance? Or would he have been with Jana instead?

So many *ifs*, and he hated to think of a life without Ruby. He'd messed up too much and for too long. He was done with that. He didn't know where he fit in with his family anymore, because things were beyond complicated between him and Holt. But being able to spend time with Ruby would be worth the other barriers he had to push through.

Somehow, the gods of Prosper heaven were smiling down on him, because the U-joint worked. Knox thanked his lucky star, whichever one it was, as the truck purred to life. He was back in business. First stop was back to the mechanic's shop so that he could buy an extra bottle of oil. As he drove, the memories of Prosper flooded back. The high school. The café where he'd hang out with his friends. The bar . . . Racoons was closed up this time of day, but he had no doubt it would be hopping as soon as the sun set. Especially with so many people in town for the rodeo.

But Knox was finished with the bar scene. The booze, the late nights, the women . . . If there was one thing his divorce taught him, it was that some mistakes couldn't ever be corrected. It took his own ex-wife marrying his brother to send the final message through Knox's stubborn brain that there were some pains that could never be dulled with drinking.

He'd never made it to his brother's wedding, but that day had become a banner day for him, and he hadn't touched alcohol since. He just wished the road hadn't been so hard to making that change in his life.

Still, his hands felt jittery as he drove past the bar. Even though he'd been clean for months, that didn't diminish the pull. The temptation. The way he knew it would make him feel—throw him into a blissful oblivion where he didn't have to dwell on how he'd been a lousy husband and even worse father to an innocent little kid.

Knox's jaw was clenched tight by the time he stopped in front of the mechanic shop. He needed to push past the haunting memories, both good and bad. He needed to exist in the present and only look toward the future.

Not Over You

As he climbed out of his truck, his phone chimed with a text. He pulled it out and glanced at the screen. He'd already told his mom he wouldn't be at the ranch for dinner, but he'd come shortly after to pick up Ruby and spend some time with her. Knox wasn't too keen on making polite conversation with Holt and Macie at the same time, with his parents looking on.

His other siblings were off, doing their things. Lane was embroiled in some high-brow graduate program. Evie was in San Antonio, doing the digital media marketing for a newspaper, and Cara was cooking up a storm at some exclusive culinary arts school. It was a wonder that Knox was even related to these folks at all. He had no aspirations for college, or for cooking, or for anything on a computer.

Which brought him back to Holt, the oldest of the family, who was the ranch manager for Prosperity Ranch. Truth be told, Knox was probably most like Holt—at least in interests for an occupation. But there was no room at the family ranch for Knox. Maybe if he'd stayed married to Macie, things might have worked out differently. But that door was completely shut, locked, and sealed now.

Inside the shop, he shook hands with the owner, Bill, and they walked out to his truck together.

"It's great to see you in town, Knox," Bill said. "We're all looking forward to the rodeo tomorrow night."

Knox dipped his head. "Thanks, man. It's always good to have someone rooting for me."

Bill chuckled. "Well, the stands will be full of fans tomorrow. I'm taking the wife and kids."

"Great to hear," Knox said.

Bill continued the small talk for a while longer. After leaving, Knox headed to the grocery store. He parked in front because the rear lot was full—with all the visitors, and whatnot.

"Oh my gosh, would you look at who's in Prosper?" a woman said when he was in one of the store's aisles.

It could have been anyone, because he didn't recognize the voice. He turned, and barely had a chance to recognize the platinum blonde hair and pink glitter shirt of Barb before she launched her arms about his neck in a hug.

Her perfume must be extra strength, because he almost choked on the smell.

She drew away from him, her bright pink lips stretched into a wide smile. "You are looking fine, Knox. I heard you were in town, but I never expected to see you at the grocery store." She laughed and peered into the basket he was carrying, containing a few essentials.

"Great to see you, Barb," Knox said, stepping back, and hoping she'd get the hint to release him.

She dropped her arms, but one hand strayed to his bicep. "So, what's new, big guy? I mean, you're single now, and tearing up the pro circuit. You must be living your best life."

Could she smile any bigger? Everyone in Prosper, and probably beyond, knew to only give Barb minimal information. "I don't know if I'd consider being divorced and not seeing my daughter much living the high life."

Barb's mouth puckered into a pout. "Oh, you poor thing. I heard all about the divorce, of course, and then she went and married your *brother* of all people." At least she'd lowered her voice, but still . . .

Knox wondered if he was in one of those B movies that populated Netflix nowadays.

"Well, Macie did what was best for her, and things are fine," he said, wanting to hightail it out of the store, even if it meant leaving his grocery basket behind.

Barb tilted her head. "You're such a sweetheart about it all," she said. "I'm so impressed." Her hand with her long pink nails remained on his arm. "I've got to confess, though, Macie and I are friends. Not best friends, mind you, but we hang out once in a while. I hope you won't be too mad about that."

"Of course, not," Knox said. "Macie's a fine woman."

At the lift of Barb's eyebrows, he took another step away.

"Sorry, I've gotta run," he said. "Great seeing you."

"You, too, Knox," Barb said. "I'll be cheering for you tomorrow night."

Knox tipped his hat but kept walking toward the cash register. *Please don't follow.*

7

"Don't be a stick in the mud," Barb said into the phone.

Jana rolled her eyes. "Just because I'm not going to the rodeo doesn't mean I'm boring."

When Barb didn't answer, Jana said, "Really? When have I *ever* gone to the rodeo?"

"Now that I think of it, it's been a long time . . . maybe since high school." Barb hummed. "Not since you and Knox—"

"Okay, that's enough of memory lane," Jana cut in. "Besides, I've got orders to fill. The raspberry jam is selling like crazy, and the stores have put in new orders."

"Whatever, hon," Barb said, not an ounce of sympathy in her voice. "Raspberries aren't going anywhere, and a couple of hours off isn't going to crash your business."

"Maybe, maybe not. But I hope you have fun," Jana said in a peppy tone. "Tell me all about it tomorrow."

Barb laughed. "All right, hon. If you change your mind . . ."

"I know, I know." Jana was smiling when she hung up, but she was also irritated.

She wasn't going to the rodeo, that was for sure, but Barb had also told her about seeing Knox at the grocery store. She'd told Jana that he was all broken up over Macie. "I think he's still in love . . . "

Yeah, that was irritating. Why exactly, Jana wasn't entirely sure, but just the thought of it brought back the emotions she'd long gotten over when she first heard about the shotgun wedding. But why should *she* feel betrayed? Those lingering feelings needed to go away, now.

Jana set to work in the kitchen. Her parents had been excited about the additional orders, but that only meant she was once again putting off her novel. After dropping off Knox at his truck yesterday afternoon, she'd gone on a major writing binge. Clocking in three chapters by the end of the night, she'd written more in one day than she could ever remember writing.

And right now, she had all kinds of ideas of how to raise the stakes in her novel. Enter a two-timing best friend and an old flame . . . Now if only Jana could write at the same time she made jam.

The evening descended faster than she was paying attention to, and only with the cooling breeze coming through the window did she realize that the rodeo had already started. She figured it wouldn't be much different than the last time she had gone to a rodeo. They'd start out with the tie-down roping.

The bull-riding was always last, which meant that there was plenty of time to make it there, if she did change her mind. Which she wasn't going to.

Jana lined up the final jars on the counter so they could cool. Both counters and the kitchen table were full of the jars of scarlet red jam. She'd be the last one to believe that Knox had been serious about learning to make jam. So why had he been so insistent?

A fluttery feeling began in her belly. Was it because he

wanted to hang out with *her*? But, why? For old time's sake? Then her face flamed. Was he looking at her as a stopover fling? Her chest burned hot. She was not that kind of woman, despite what had happened between them in high school. She'd been . . . caught in the moment, she guessed. In awe that the most popular guy in school had singled her out.

But it wasn't just his looks and charm—it was the way they were around each other. He listened. He understood. Her sister's ambitions were a lot like his siblings, whereas the two of them weren't college-bound. They had things in common—their sense of humor, how they could be laughing at one moment, then walking hand-in-hand the next without speaking a word. They'd been comfortable with each other.

That was it. Jana had been comfortable with him. Had trusted him. And she supposed, there'd been some rebellion in her, as well as bright stars in her eyes. She believed Knox when he said he'd make it big, that he'd travel the country riding bulls, that he'd make a name for himself.

All that had happened . . . just without her, and with plenty of broken baggage on the way there.

Whatever his intentions were about making jam with her, it wasn't going to happen. No way. But did that mean she couldn't watch him do what he did best?

Jana glanced at the kitchen clock. The rodeo would be in full swing now. If she showered quickly, and put her hair up in a ponytail or something, she could still catch the end of it. She probably wouldn't even have to buy a ticket.

That was how she found herself driving to the arena thirty minutes later, her heart thumping, her mind changing every five seconds. There was literally no place to park, so she ended up walking a good fifteen minutes to get to the arena. Sure enough, the ticket booths were closed, so she walked in.

The announcer was going crazy over a rider named

Devon on a bull called Big Chance. Maybe Knox had already gone? Jana climbed up the stands and found a seat on the very top row that looked like it had been abandoned. She had no idea where Barb and Patsy were sitting. She planned to leave before the thing ended, anyway.

"And there he goes, folks," the announcer boomed. "Down before the eight seconds, but what a ride. Let's give Devon some appreciation for a tough battle."

Jana clapped along with the rest of the spectators. Another bull-rider came out on a black beast that looked like he was ready to kill something. He bucked his way toward the edge of the arena, and the spectators hanging close to the walls squealed and moved back.

"Watch your fingers and toes," the announcer said with a chuckle. "Black Volcano means business tonight, yessir."

When the cowboy atop the bull was tossed to the ground, the spectators groaned. "Tough luck, folks. Sometimes, the bull is just too mighty even for a seasoned rider."

Two more riders on two more bulls. From her perspective, she couldn't tell who was waiting to ride next until the rider climbed up the side of the gate and straddled the bull.

"Next up is our hometown favorite," the announcer boomed. Cheers started before he said, "Let's welcome Knox Prosper back to our rodeo!"

The stands went nuts, and half of the people were on their feet clapping and yelling.

Jana's skin buzzed at the amazing reception. Knox truly was everyone's cowboy, and she was pretty sure after tonight, he'd forget all about her—Jana Harris and her small life.

She could only see his back and his cowboy hat from her seat, but the power of the bull beneath him was tangible. It was already pushing against the gate. And then the gate flew open, and out went Knox.

Not Over You

"Look at him go! If anyone can ride King Pin, it's Knox Prosper!"

The crowd was on their feet, clapping and yelling. Jana jumped to her feet, then stood on her seat in the last row. Finally, she had a decent view. Knox was hanging on tight, and she thought of the fundamentals he'd told her about riding. Forward on the jump. Yep, he had that down. It was as if he were surfing an ocean wave by the way he moved with the bull, keeping in control of his balance. And the intangibles—feel and effort. That was what kept Knox winning, she was sure of it.

He'd told her every bull was different. And King Pin was huge and muscled and on a terror streak. The noise from the crowd only increased as they counted the seconds. Knox held on fast, and when the buzzer went off, the crowd roared. He eased his grip on the bull and slid off.

Both relief and adrenaline shot through Jana. He'd done it, and he was okay. No injuries.

"And there you have it, folks," the announcer boomed. "Bull-riding at its finest by our own Knox Prosper!"

As if to answer, Knox took off his helmet, then waved it at the crowd, and the fans responded with enthusiasm.

"Let's see what the judges say about Knox's ride," the announcer continued. The seconds ticked by while the announcer read through some of Knox's previous scores at other rodeos. "This just in. Looks like Knox Prosper is getting an even 96. This puts him in the lead for the night. Congratulations, young man!"

Whistles sounded around Jana, and she found herself grinning and clapping. The next two bull-riders didn't come close to Knox's score, and the arena buzzed in anticipation of Knox staying on top. It seemed that his thousands of fans were only too happy to celebrate with him.

Jana should really leave right now if she wanted to get ahead of the crowd, but she didn't move. For some reason, she felt mesmerized by the lights against the dark night, the glittering stars above, the warm summer breeze, and the thrum of energy from the people.

After the rodeo came to a close, Jana still remained in her seat while people filed out of the stands. The place emptied slowly, as the crowds funneled through the narrow exits. Jana supposed the cowboys were all in the lot behind the arena, taking care of their animals. The maintenance crew started up, cleaning up the garbage in the stands, and plowing the dirt in the arena.

Only when the crew neared her row did Jana get up and walk down the stairs. She headed out of the arena, folding her arms against the cooling night. Most of the cars and trucks were gone now, and she still had a ways to walk. Her steps slowed when she looked over to the parking lot with a few horse trailers left. Cowboys had congregated into groups, talking.

When a certain cowboy caught her eye, her breath stalled.

Knox was talking to his family from the looks of it. Macie, Holt, their mother Heidi, and the mayor, Rex Prosper.

In Knox's arms, he held a little girl who had to be Ruby. Jana had seen Ruby briefly once or twice about town, but she'd never officially met her.

It seemed that Knox was plenty busy, and Jana continued walking, her heart clenching a little. How hard must it be for Knox to be around his family now that his ex was married to his brother? Had Barb been right? Did Knox still have feelings for Macie?

Jana shook away the thoughts. It wasn't any of her business to speculate or to even care about it. She hurried to her

SUV, waving at a few vehicles that slowed—she didn't really recognize anyone in the dark.

Texts started piling in from Barb about the rodeo being over, about Knox winning the bull-riding, and how everyone was heading to Racoons.

We can pick you up, or you can meet us there, Barb had texted.

Jana was debating whether she should tell Barb about coming to the rodeo after all when another truck slowed behind her. She was far enough on the side of the road to let it pass, but the truck didn't pass her.

"I thought that was you," a deep, familiar voice said.

Jana's pulse doubled, and she looked over to see Knox driving. No one was with him, which surprised her, although she wasn't sure why. Maybe because she thought he'd be with his family, going somewhere to celebrate his win?

Since Knox had pulled to a stop, she stopped, too.

"Changed your mind about coming to the rodeo?" Knox teased.

How could he look so . . . great? He should be a sweaty, dirty mess, but he only exuded masculinity.

Jana moved closer to the truck, while still keeping a fair distance. "Thought I'd see what all the fuss was about."

He chuckled. "And what did you think, sweetheart?"

The endearment shouldn't have affected her; it was common enough around these parts. But she felt her pulse go up another notch. "Impressive," she said, a smile tugging at her mouth. "I guess congratulations are in order."

Knox tapped the brim of his hat. "If you're doling them out, then I'm accepting, ma'am."

"Oh, so modest," Jana teased. "I see not much has changed about Knox Prosper after all."

"Well, between you and me," he said in a low tone, "I didn't want to change the good parts."

The heat in her chest inched up her neck. Jana stepped back. "Well, congratulations again, and good luck again tomorrow night."

"Want a ride?"

"My car's just up there," Jana said, pointing, although it wasn't exactly visible in the darkness.

"Want a ride?" Knox said, his tone low and warm.

Jana hesitated, then took a step toward the truck, and Knox leaned over to pop open the door for her. She climbed in, her heart in her throat, her hands too hot. She smoothed them over her black jeans she'd paired with a blue and white polka-dotted shirt.

Knox began to drive, slowly, because her car was only a half-block up ahead.

Jana dared another glance at him. "Heading to a big celebration with your family?"

"Nah," he said. "There's another night of bull-riding to go. Besides, the only one I wanted to spend time with is Ruby, but there's a lot of factors involved."

"She's darling," Jana blurted out, hoping it was okay to say. The little girl obviously took after her mom with her dark curls and brown eyes.

Knox only smiled. "She's got every member of the Prosper family wrapped twice around her pinkie finger."

"I'll bet," Jana said. "First grandkid, and all." She bit her lip, not knowing what was off-limits here.

Knox was already slowing the truck because they'd reached her SUV. Her phone chimed three times in a row, as if the texts had waited to deliver at the same moment.

"Busy night?" Knox said.

Jana glanced down at her phone. "It's Barb. The ladies are meeting at Racoons, with half the town, I imagine."

"Well, have fun."

His tone was kind of off, and Jana met his eyes. Even in the dim light of the dashboard, she could feel the intensity of his gaze.

"You going?" she said. "I'm sure you'll get free drinks all night."

"Naw," he said. "I'm done with the bar scene. Stirred up too much trouble in my life."

Jana blinked. "Wow, I didn't know. I mean, the place is harmless, really. No bar fights around here or crazy stuff going on."

Knox took off his cowboy hat and scrubbed a hand over his hair. It was a wild mess, but sexy, too, as one would expect. "I've been dry for eight months now. So being in a bar complicates things."

"Oh, yeah, true." Jana couldn't stop staring at him. He'd given up bars and didn't drink?

"Like I said, Jana Harris, I'm a changed man."

Jana nodded, her mind spinning too fast to respond.

"And if you're okay with that, maybe you'd agree to have lunch with me tomorrow?" he said, one edge of his mouth lifting. "Or better yet, I could bring lunch to your place, and you can teach me all about jam-making."

Jana was still trying to process what Knox had told her about not going to bars. It took her a moment to say, "You don't give up easily, do you?"

"No, ma'am." Knox held her gaze. "You still got my number?"

"I do." She held back a smile and climbed out. "Thanks for the ride."

"Anytime."

8

KNOX WAITED UNTIL Jana got in her car and pulled out before he stepped on the gas again. But then she braked in front of him, so he braked, too. He couldn't have been more surprised than he was seeing her climb out and walk toward his truck. Her black jeans followed her curves to a T, and her hair hung in waves down her back. Waves he'd been tempted to touch when she was sitting next to him in the truck. His windows were already down, and when she reached his side, she rested her fingers on the windowsill.

"Where are you headed?" she asked.

Again, he was surprised. "Heading to the truck stop for a shower and some grub, then I think I'll call it a night."

"You're sleeping in your truck again?"

"That's correct."

"Because it's less complicated that way?"

A chuckle escaped. "Correct again. Changed your mind about lunch tomorrow?"

"No," she said, then leaned in a little closer. "But I've got a free shower and two extra bedrooms. Or a couch. Whichever you prefer. Just don't expect anything fancy to eat."

Knox couldn't help the grin that emerged, although he really should say no. He knew he wouldn't sleep much a wall or two away from a beautiful woman such as Jana. Even if he'd sworn off his past indulgences.

"I'd be crazy to turn down an offer like that," he said. "But I don't want to impose, or, uh, start any tongues wagging. Besides, what would your boyfriend think?" He was almost positive she didn't have one, or wouldn't he have seen signs of the guy by now?

"I don't have a boyfriend to chase away, so don't worry about that, Mr. Prosper." Her smile was soft, teasing. "No one in the town has to know unless you tell them."

"I think it would be pretty obvious if my truck is parked at your place, sweetheart." His hand strayed to the fingers resting on his windowsill. Her fingers were warm, and her skin smooth.

She didn't pull her hands away, even though her brows lifted. "So park your truck somewhere, and we'll take my SUV."

Knox could do this, stay the next night or two at the Harris house. No big deal. He and Jana were in the past. Now, they were . . . friends? "You got a deal."

Jana nodded and stepped away from the truck. She was smiling, and he was, too. *Easy, cowboy.* There were about a hundred complications between them already, and first one up was that Knox didn't want to jump into anything too fast. Things with Macie had . . . wrecked him. And he didn't want bad decisions and stress to send him down another dark path.

But his thumping heart wasn't listening as he pulled over to the side of the road. Parked. He snatched his duffle bag, then climbed out and made his way to Jana's SUV.

Once inside, he found that his heart was racing much too fast for his liking. This was nothing, he told himself. Just some neighborly hospitality. By the time they pulled up to Jana's house, every part of his body felt jittery. He'd shower, eat a

Not Over You

sandwich or something—a jam sandwich—then call it a night. And hope to heaven, he'd fall asleep quickly.

The inside of the house smelled amazing. The signs of jam-making were cleaned up, but the sweet scent of fruit remained.

"Want some water?" Jana went to the fridge to pull out a pitcher of cold water.

After pouring him a glass, he told her, "You don't have to wait on me. Just point me to the shower."

She took a sip of her water, then said, "First door on the right. I'll have dinner ready when you're out." Then she stifled a yawn.

"Really, Jana, I can fix a sandwich or something."

"Off with you." She waved him toward the hallway.

So he finished the water, then headed to the shower. By the time he returned to the kitchen, there was a new aroma. That of something delicious.

Jana was at the stove, frying up hamburger. On the counter, she had small bowls of different things like diced tomatoes, shredded cheese, and torn lettuce.

"You're cooking?" Knox said as he crossed to the stove.

Jana glanced over at him, then returned to stirring the sizzling meat. "Making tacos. Hope you're not allergic."

"Now, who in their right mind would be allergic to tacos?" Knox said, bracing his hands on the counter next to the stove. "What can I help with?"

Another glance at him, and he wondered if the flush of her cheeks was from the heat of the stove. She'd taken off her boots, but she still wore the black jeans and blue shirt. "You can set the table. The plates are in that cupboard." She nodded toward the cupboard closest to him.

He set the table quickly, then carried over the bowls with the various toppings.

When Jana brought over the meat scooped into a bowl, she sat across from him.

"This is right nice, Jana," Knox started, "but—"

"Just say thank you," she cut in with a smile. "You act as if no one ever did anything nice for you."

Knox chuckled. "All right. I'll shut up and eat." He winked at her.

Then he dug in, and it was amazing. Maybe he was just hungry, but he'd never had better tacos. When he was on his second taco, he said, "Is there anything you can't do, Ms. Harris?"

Jana smirked, and that playful look in her eyes reminded him of years ago, when they'd always seemed to have fun together, even when they were doing nothing.

"I can't ride a bull," she said.

"Have you ever tried?"

"No . . ."

He leaned forward and lowered his voice. "Then how do you know you can't do it unless you've tried?"

"Oh, you're funny," Jana said, picking up her water glass. "Not all of us are as crazy as you."

Knox sat back and surveyed her. "Women bull-ride."

"Women who are as tough as nails and built of muscle," she said. "I'm none of that."

"Your body would get used to it soon enough," he said with a shrug. "Once you learn the techniques, it's just reflex."

"Sorry, Knox," she said, her eyes gleaming with amusement as she pulled a lock of her hair forward and twisted it around her fingers, "you're not even speaking my language. Tonight was the first night I've even stepped foot in a rodeo arena since, well, since high school. It might be another seven years before I go again."

"That's too bad, sweetheart, because I was hoping for a repeat tomorrow night."

Jana's brows lifted. "Why, you gonna win again?"

"I can almost guarantee it." He wasn't being cocky, just honest.

But Jana laughed.

"What's so funny?" Knox asked.

She just shook her head and returned to her food.

"So . . . I've been curious about something," he said when he'd finished a third taco and was finally feeling satisfied.

Jana looked at him, giving him her full attention.

"Why don't you have a boyfriend?" he asked.

She hesitated at this, her hazel eyes flickering away for a second. "There's always some big thing, I guess. I mean, I get asked out on dates, but they don't progress too much. Also, I'm happy in Prosper, and there's not much selection here. I really couldn't imagine dating someone I knew in high school. It would be like dating my brother, if I had a brother."

"You dated me."

Jana's cheeks pinked. "Well, you were different. But you moved on. Everyone moved on. Maybe my cowboy is just biding his time before he snatches me up."

"Maybe." Knox couldn't look away from her. He was pretty sure she had the exact number of freckles she had in high school.

Jana stood from the table and began to clear things off. So Knox rose, too, and helped her. As she started to wash the dishes, he joined her at the sink and said, "Let me do that."

She peered up at him, and he wanted to lean down and breathe in her raspberry scent. Not a raspberry in sight, yet she still smelled sweet.

"How about you dry?" she said. "I'm sure you're beat and

want to get to bed." Her gaze flitted away, and she filled one side of the sink with soapy water.

"It always takes me a while to fall asleep after a rodeo," he said. "But a full stomach will certainly help."

She nodded as she handed him the newly scrubbed frying pan. "So I've been wondering something about you, too."

"Oh, what's that, sweetheart?"

"What are you going to do after bull-riding?"

He looked over at her. "You thinking my days are numbered?"

"No," she said quickly. "I mean, bull-riding is what, five, ten years? Then what?"

"I don't rightly know, because Holt's running the ranch for my dad, so that kind of cancels me out," he said. "Maybe, I'll go to college."

Jana scoffed. "You're kidding."

"What?" He laughed. "You don't think I can pass the classes?"

She finished up the last dish and handed it over, then drained the water from the sink. "I think you could pass any class you set your mind to, but I just can't picture you mixing with college people." She grabbed another dish towel and dried her hands.

"Yeah, you're probably right," he said, drying the final dish. "I've been thinking about making jam."

Jana snapped a dish towel at him, and he dodged out of the way with a laugh.

"Careful with that," he said. "You're gonna make me drop this plate."

She backed away, a smile on her face. "I need some sort of defense being around you."

He set the plate in the cupboard, then walked toward her.

Not Over You

She continued to move around the table, keeping the distance even between them.

"What about you, ma'am?" he asked. "Are you going to work for your parents the rest of your life?"

"No . . . I have plans."

"Your column? Taking it big? You never did tell me what your column is about."

"It's a dating advice column," she said, looking a bit wary of how he'd react.

"I should probably read that," he said with a wink, moving closer. "You know, get some tips."

Jana shrugged. "You never know. But I'm also writing a novel—hoping to get it published someday. In fact, it's my third book. I just need to find the right publisher."

Knox stopped in his tracks. "Wow, that's amazing. Why am I not surprised? You always were the smartest girl I knew."

She folded her arms and bit the edge of her lip. "You mean my sister was. She's the one with the law degree."

"Yeah, but I don't know her."

Jana's smile was slow and beautiful. Like the rest of her. She moved toward the hallway. "Well, good night, Knox. Help yourself to whatever you need, but turn the lights out when you go to bed."

With that, she disappeared down the hallway.

Knox could have talked to her all night, but it seemed that Jana was the wiser out of the two.

He had been right about one thing. It took him a long time to fall asleep.

9

JANA WAS SURPRISED she'd slept at all the night before. She was pretty sure Knox went to bed soon after her—at least, she didn't hear any sounds about the house. But when she awakened, the house was completely silent. Which was a good thing. She could shower and be ready before he woke up.

She crept out of bed, listening for any signs of Knox being awake. After her shower, the house was still silent, and she chanced a walk by the bedroom he'd chosen—Natalie's, as opposed to her parents'.

The door wasn't shut all the way, allowing for a sliver to see into the room. Although Jana slowed her step, she wasn't about to peek in on him. So she continued toward the kitchen. She'd make two batches of jam today before pickup, then she planned on devoting the afternoon and evening to her book. She was caught up on a week's worth of columns, anyway.

She debated whether to make breakfast for Knox. Would he be sleeping in? Or would he be heading to the rodeo grounds as soon as he woke up?

She cracked a few eggs into the frying pan and set the burner on medium. Then she made a fresh batch of orange juice. She didn't have bacon or hash browns, so Knox would have to be grateful for what he got. Which he had been so far . . .

Which brought her thoughts circling to the fact that her ex-boyfriend had spent the night in her house. And . . . they'd been cordial. All right, more than cordial. Friendly, and maybe a tad flirty. She exhaled and flipped the eggs. The other sides of the eggs sizzled while she poured herself a glass of orange juice.

Knox would be leaving tomorrow, and who knew when she'd see him again. Sure, he'd come into town to see his daughter, but not Jana. Unless he needed a place to stay again? She grimaced. He'd stay at the bed and breakfast, since the rodeo crowd would be gone.

She spent the next hour preparing the jars and canning more raspberry jam. While the jars were in the water canner, she brought her laptop to the kitchen table to finish the scene she'd started the day before. She read through what she'd written, and that's when she realized she was nearly to the first kiss between the hero and heroine. Right now in the story, Ryan and Sandy were in New York and were working late hours on a business deal together at a marketing company. They'd been friends for a couple of years, but Sandy's boyfriend had stopped Ryan from asking Sandy out.

But now that Sandy was a free woman, Ryan was testing the waters a little. The sun had set, and the shadows had turned purple in the conference room. Ryan ordered in dinner, and Sandy was glued to the computer making adjustments on their digital design. When dinner arrived, they began to eat, and the conversation turned flirty—very flirty.

Jana was smiling as she typed, totally absorbed in the scene, when a voice spoke close to her ear. "Ryan, huh? He's got some moves."

Not Over You

Jana yelped, closed the laptop cover, and placed a hand over her chest. "You scared me. Don't do that again!"

Knox chuckled.

He still stood behind her, and he leaned forward, then opened the laptop screen. "Why'd you shut it?"

She shoved his hand away. "No, you don't."

He was still behind her, and so close she felt his warm breath against her neck. Ignoring the goose bumps racing across her skin from his scent of soap and pine, she rose, careful to move away from him as she did so. Then she tucked the laptop under her arm and turned to face him.

Oh boy.

Knox was wearing a fitted T-shirt and jeans. His dark blonde hair was damp from a shower, and his whiskers only made him look more handsome.

"You're seriously not going to let me read your book?"

Jana knew she was blushing, but she didn't care. She took another step back. "It's a romance novel, if you have to know, and you're not exactly my target audience."

He merely smiled and folded those tanned arms of his, which only made her heart skip another beat. The full force of allowing Knox Prosper to sleep in her house last night was starting to hit her. He was dang sexy in the morning. She needed to keep her distance, and she needed to change the topic. She moved around the table, still clutching her laptop. "Made you some breakfast."

His gaze cut to the counter, where she'd piled the eggs on a plate and covered it. "Jana, you're an angel."

While he brought the plate to the table, she slipped into the living room to set the laptop in there. When she returned, Knox was halfway through his eggs.

"Want some orange juice?" she asked. Staying busy would be good.

"Love some."

She brought over a tall glass of juice, then set about checking the jam in the water canners, even though she knew they weren't finished.

When Knox finished his breakfast, he washed his dishes, then moved to where she was checking her phone for any delivery notifications. Nothing had come in, so she figured the pickup would be the same time this afternoon. It was nearly ten in the morning now. But she couldn't ignore him when he was standing so close, watching her.

"What?" she asked, looking up at him.

Knox smiled as he shook his head. "How many people have you let read your book?"

This was not what she expected. "Um, a few people have."

"Who?"

She pocketed her phone. "Um . . ."

He nodded. "That's what I thought. Tell me about it." The green of his eyes seemed to bore into her.

"Well, it's boy meets girl, they realize they're perfect for each other, and they live happily ever after. You know, all the standard stuff."

"Doesn't sound standard to me," he said, "at least in my experience."

He was still too close, even though there were about three feet between them.

"Maybe it's not standard in real life," Jana said, "but books are supposed to be a break from real life. A getaway."

"If anyone needs a getaway in life, it's me." His mouth twitched.

"What's so bad about your life?" she teased.

"Well . . ." He pretended to think. "I wasted a lot of years being mad at someone I shouldn't have ever been mad at."

Jana's pulse rose . . . He was going *there*?

He leaned against the counter, not too far away from her. "Then I thought getting married was the right thing to do—and maybe it was—but I had a lot of growing up to do still. So I really worked that angle and dumped my family and stepped out on my wife."

Jana went very, very still.

But Knox's voice was even, calm, like he was telling someone else's story. "Then I try to work out visitation with Ruby, and it's always on her mom's schedule, never mine. Not to mention every time I want to see my kid, I have to face the fact that my ex-wife is now my sister-in-law. It's like my family is too crowded for me to fit in it anymore. Not that I can blame anyone. I was pretty rotten."

Jana could only stare at him. She didn't know what to say—she hadn't expected him to be so open about all of this.

"So, don't you think I deserve to read a happily-ever-after story?" His green eyes held hers. "A *getaway* book?"

"That's quite the sob story, Mr. Bull-Rider."

"It's not over yet," he said.

"Oh? Do continue."

He took a step closer, raised his hand, and touched her hair. Then his hand skimmed her shoulder before it dropped.

Jana wasn't sure if she was able to take a full breath.

"I've had to get over some pretty bad habits—on some days, I didn't know if I was coming or going. But most of all, I've got a lot of regrets . . . especially with you."

Jana had no answer, and she didn't know if she'd be able to speak even if she did.

"So . . . does that buy me access to your book?"

She couldn't help but laugh. "You're one persistent man."

"That I am." He was giving her one of those heart-stopping smiles.

"Okay, one chapter."

He grinned and strode to the living room.

"Wait," she called after him, hurrying to join him.

He sat on the couch and handed her the laptop.

"I can't believe you," she mumbled, but she couldn't deny the thrill running through her. She was both thrilled and a little petrified. She opened the laptop, then scrolled to the top of the manuscript.

"Read it to me," he said, and then he draped an arm across the back of the couch. His arm wasn't touching her, but he was definitely increasing his presence.

Heat crawled up her neck as she began, but she continued, trying not to be self-conscious about her writing. Yet, she wondered the whole time what he thought of it. When she finished the first chapter, she closed the laptop.

"That's it?" he asked. "I'm waiting to see what happens with Sandy's job promotion."

"Spoiler. She gets the job."

"Ah, good to know. And her loser boyfriend? Is she going to start taking Ryan seriously? He's the one treating her right."

"You're pretty good at catching all the foreshadowing."

His brows furrowed. "What shadows?"

"You know." She elbowed him. "The plot device we talked about in English class. Where the author leaves a clue of what's to come."

"I still have no idea, but I believe you," he said. "You paid a lot more attention in that class. I think I spent most of my time paying attention to *you*."

Jana wouldn't allow herself to blush. "When you say things like that, it makes me think you're flirting with me. And we're both past that." She was pretty sure she'd shocked him, but he merely turned toward her.

"You know . . . since my divorce, I've done a lot of thinking." He paused. "I've gone about a lot of stuff wrong in my life, and I hope to correct that one thing at a time. Might take me forever, but it's all I can hang onto for now."

"What are you trying to correct?"

"Flirting with women who I know I don't want to end up with," he said.

"So . . . I'm a special case?"

He didn't answer at first, then surprisingly, he moved to his feet. "You've always been special, Jana. I don't think I appreciated it as much as I should have, though." He extended his hand.

Now, it was Jana's turn to hesitate.

"I won't bite, promise."

She placed her hand in his larger, warmer one. She ignored the appearance of her trusty goose bumps and rose to her feet easily with Knox's help. He didn't release her hand, but rubbed his thumb over her wrist.

Tingles zoomed up her arm, and she wanted to lean into him, press her cheek against his T-shirt. Feel his arms about her. But his sweet words and regretful tone wouldn't make her a fool twice.

"Well, thanks for listening to my chapter," she said, pulling her hand away even though it was the last thing she wanted to do. "The jam should be done now, so back to work."

"Best story time I've ever been to," Knox said as he followed her into the kitchen.

She turned off the water canners, then lifted their lids. Steam billowed out, the moisture clouding over her.

"What can I help with?" Knox asked.

She hesitated, and he noticed it.

"I'm serious, I don't have to be anywhere for a couple of hours, so I'm all yours," he said. "Unless you're sick of me? You can kick me out, you know."

She glanced over to see his beautiful smile. She might

have melted just a bit. "All right. I'm going to let these jars cool before setting them on the table. But in the meantime, we can prepare the next batch." She snatched an apron off the hook on the pantry door. "You're going to need this."

He dutifully tied on the apron as she tied on hers, and soon, they were standing side by side, washing raspberries she'd fetched from cold storage.

"See, I'm already an expert," Knox teased.

Standing so close to him was making her pulse rise again, because they were doing something so domesticated . . . like they were best friends. Or something more.

"Now comes the measuring, then the smashing of the fruit."

"You do it by hand?"

"Of course," she said. "We're not called Harris Farms for nothing. We're homemade all the way."

"Good enough for me." Knox used the potato masher to do the raspberries justice.

When he was finished, Jana added the rest of the ingredients. "Now, we pour." She demonstrated how much of the jam concoction should be poured into each jar. Then she added the sterilized lids.

"Am I doing this right?" Knox asked.

"Yeah, except you're not supposed to drip the jam over the edge."

"Whoops." He set down the bowl and used his finger to swipe at the stray drip.

"Here, use this wet paper towel," she said. "It's more sanitary."

"Ah, thanks." Knox used the paper towel, but for the next jars, he suddenly turned into a perfectionist and didn't spill anything. "Yes! Do you see this jar? Not one drip."

"Nice," Jana said, keeping the laughter out of her tone, because he was like an excited kid.

The work went twice as fast even though she had to take the time to explain things. Soon, the new jars were in the pressure cookers, and the first set of jars had finished cooling and Knox had loaded them into boxes.

"How long do they sit in the water canner?"

"About fifteen minutes."

Knox nodded. "And when does the delivery man come to pick them up?"

"Not until 4:00 today."

"So you have a few hours to spare?"

Jana set her hands on her hips. "Maybe..."

Knox rose from where he was sitting at the table and walked toward her where she'd just set the water canner timers. The kitchen was plenty warm, but his gaze on her was making her hot.

"Do you want to come to the park with me?" he asked when he stopped close to her. "I'm picking up Ruby in about an hour, and I thought maybe..."

She raised her brows, waiting. "Maybe what?"

"Maybe if you want to get out of the house, you'd like to come," he said. "Or you can bring your laptop, and you know, write in nature. Get some inspiration."

"The story takes place in New York City."

"Right." But he was smiling, and he must know that his smile did funny things to her mind, because she found herself considering it.

"The park is very public," she said.

Knox shrugged. "Well, now that I know you don't have a boyfriend, I'm good with a little gossip."

"Oh, really?" Jana laughed. "That's all it took, huh?"

His fingers slid over hers, then he grasped her hand.

The kitchen was definitely a too-hot place to be with a man like Knox Prosper.

"Please?"

She placed a hand on his chest, fully intending on pushing him away, and telling him she'd think about it. But somehow, her hand moved from his chest up and over his shoulder, bringing their bodies flush.

Knox's eyes seemed to darken, and Jana was pretty sure her heart was doing somersaults.

"Why do you want me to come?"

He didn't seem surprised at her question, and he also didn't hesitate. "Because I want my daughter to meet my friend."

Jana felt a smile tug at the edges of her mouth. "So, we're friends now?"

"You bet." He winked, sufficiently distracting her from the fact that his other hand had slid around her waist. They couldn't get much closer unless they were, in fact, kissing. Which probably shouldn't happen.

Knox had been open and honest with her, and she'd held back pretty much everything . . . her own regrets, and her continued crush on him. It was probably way more than a crush, especially now that they'd cleared the air between them, but she couldn't overlook the complications, either.

"Knox, what are we doing?"

She didn't need to explain further, because he released her then. His brow furrowed, and she didn't like it one bit.

Scrubbing a hand through his hair, he said, "I'm not gonna lie, I'm wishing right now that I didn't have to leave tomorrow. You're unexpected, Jana. I thought we'd have an argument about the past and I'd never see you again—unless by chance. But now . . . my mind is spinning with all sorts of questions and possibilities."

Not Over You

She folded her arms because it stopped her from reaching for him. "Like what?" she asked in a soft voice.

He closed his eyes for a moment, and she didn't miss the torment that flittered across his expression. When he opened his eyes again, they didn't stray from her. "Like coming home to Prosper might be a possibility after all. That there might be a new beginning here for me." He ran a hand over his jaw. "With Holt married to Macie, this town has seemed too small. But if I had my own . . . life . . ."

He didn't finish, and he didn't have to. Jana didn't know if she could take much more, anyway. She was feeling overwhelmed enough. Placing her hand on her chest, even though it would do nothing to calm her racing heart, she said, "I'm glad you can see a future here, because I really like Prosper."

Had she said too much? Confessed too much? Well, Knox didn't seem to mind, because he stepped close again, and this time, his touch wasn't tentative. His hands settled on her hips, and he drew her close.

"Jana . . ." he whispered before he leaned down and pressed his mouth against hers.

His lips were warm and soft, and she wasn't sure she was still in reality. Knox was kissing her. *Kissing* her. The scrape of his whiskers against her chin only made her want to drag him closer. Her fingers curled into his shirt, and she marveled at all that had happened over the years, yet, here they were again.

"You taste like raspberries," he murmured, his mouth moving to her jaw, then her neck, and she could feel his smile against her skin.

She smiled in return and whispered, "You do, too."

He chuckled, and then his mouth was on hers again, his kissing deeper, more intense, as one hand tangled in her hair.

She didn't mind Knox kissing her, not in the least. In fact, she'd probably been anticipating—or at least hoping for—this the moment she realized the cowboy she'd pulled over to help on the side of the road was Knox Prosper. Not that she assumed, but now that he was here, in her kitchen, kissing her like he meant something by it, she was going to let him know she'd be more than happy if he moved back to Prosper.

Jana slid her hands up his chest; the warmth and the rapid beating of his heart only stirred her up more. She memorized his taste, his smell, his touch, not knowing if this thing with Knox would turn into anything real, but right here, right now, it was very real.

10

KNOX SLOWED HIS truck in front of Prosperity Ranch, and as expected, the memories of his youth came roaring back. Some good, some not so good, especially the way things had ended with his family several years ago. He still remembered the night he and his dad had gotten into a big argument—Christmastime. Macie was pregnant, and they'd been married only a few months. His dad had finally consented to hand over Knox's share of the farm in cash.

But the animosity had been stifling. What happened to being encouraged as a kid to follow his dreams? Apparently, that had applied only to everyone else in the family. Yet, he knew now it had all been a mistake. If he hadn't cut himself off from his family, would he have gone down such a dark path? Would he have destroyed his marriage? Would he have been in the position he was now? Being only a visitor to the ranch to pick up his daughter for a couple of hours?

All these thoughts surfaced, and they'd surfaced before, yet, now . . . the sting wasn't so sharp. The teeth of regret weren't sinking so hard into his skin. He felt . . . lighter, somehow. Like some of the weight had been lifted.

His daughter was happy. She was surrounded by doting

grandparents, her mom, her stepdad, her aunts and uncles. Ruby was healthy. She was as smart as a whip. And Macie... after all the turmoil of their marriage, and all the pain of the divorce, she'd found happiness. Should he begrudge that it was with his brother?

No...

And Knox... spending time with Jana had been good for both his heart and his soul. He could see that now. Talking to her, making jam with her, listening to her read her book, laughing with her . . . it had been a balm. Like a vacation, really. One sorely needed.

And that kiss . . . wow. He'd had to force himself to step back after a few minutes of indulging. Because Jana was a beautiful woman, and her scent, touch, and taste were all intoxicating. There was no doubt that she was the real deal, and the last thing he wanted to do was mess things up, or hurt her.

He was done hurting people.

Which was why he wouldn't stay at her house tonight. Their kiss had changed everything, and he hoped that she wasn't freaked out or anything. He hoped she knew he wasn't playing the field. No, he was done with that life for good.

He wanted what his parents had, what Macie and Holt had, what he believed his sister Evie had with her boyfriend. And he knew it took a lot of hard work and a lot of trust. He never wanted to betray another person's trust again.

"Daddy!" a little voice shouted.

He looked toward the barn to see Ruby running out, her grandpa close behind.

Knox's dad, Rex, had been the mayor of Prosper for many years, but he also had no problem putting in a day's work on the ranch. Beyond the barn was the training arena

Not Over You

where Holt brought in horses that needed training or other types of care. Holt's truck wasn't around, so maybe he was off on an errand. Which was just fine with Knox.

He climbed out of the truck and smiled at Ruby. "Hey there, baby. You ready to go have some fun?"

Ruby kept running, and behind her, Rex chuckled. "You sure you're ready to handle this spitfire?"

Just then, Ruby launched herself at Knox. He hoisted her up and hugged her tight.

"Any words of advice, Gramps?" Knox said, smiling at his dad. He loved that he and his dad had patched things up, and they could have conversations like this.

"I've heard it said that this particular little girl likes ice cream."

"I *do*!" Ruby said. "I love it so much, Daddy."

Knox chuckled. "Then we'll have to get you some." He carried her to the passenger side of the truck. After buckling her in and closing the door, he found his dad still standing there.

"You're looking happy, son."

Knox dipped his chin. "Time with Ruby must bring it out."

His dad nodded. "Yeah, likely. Might be something else, too."

"Won the bull-riding last night."

Rex chuckled. "That's a typical night for you."

This was a compliment coming from his dad, because Knox's passion for following his dream had been a sore point between them. "It was great all the same."

Rex clapped a hand on Knox's shoulder, but his gaze studied him. "I'll figure it out."

Knox adjusted his hat. "I'm putting a few ghosts to rest, I guess."

"Good for you," Rex said. "I mean it, son."

"Thanks." And Knox meant it, too.

Ruby began tapping on her window, then waving madly for him to get in the truck.

"Looks like I'm being summoned," Knox said. "We'll be back in a couple of hours if anyone is asking."

"Enjoy yourselves," Rex said with a wave to Ruby.

The drive to the park was filled with about eighty-four questions about bull-riding. He thought he'd answered them all the night before when he talked with his family before coming across Jana walking to her car. Apparently, Ruby still had more.

"Do the bulls get sad?"

"What do they eat?"

"Do they like ice cream?"

"Can I pet a baby bull?"

"How old are you, Daddy?"

"What's your favorite color?"

"Do you like sparkles?"

Okay, so not all of the questions were bull-riding related. By the time they reached the park and pulled into a spot near the swings, Knox wondered if anyone had ever been so thoroughly interrogated. He opened his door and climbed out, trying not to feel disappointed that Jana hadn't come with him. She said she might meet him here, but Knox was positive that was a polite way of saying no.

Ruby made a beeline for the swings, and for a second, Knox wondered what she was allowed or not allowed to do on the jungle gym. What if she fell off something or got hurt somehow? A few teens were on the other side of the park throwing a frisbee, but there weren't any other little kids around. It was just as well. Another citizen of Prosper would have asked him even more questions than Ruby.

"Daddy, push me!" Ruby called as she inched her way onto a swing.

Knox chuckled and headed over to push her on the swing, not too high, even though she kept demanding it. As a baby, Ruby had been a fussy kid, and always wanted her mom. Knox didn't blame her. But now, she was like a little person, and his heart overflowed when he was around her, and ached when he wasn't.

"Higher, Daddy."

"No, baby girl," he said. "This is high enough. I don't want you to get dizzy, because then you'll be too sick for ice cream."

"Okay." She began to sing a random song he'd never heard of.

Knox exhaled, enjoying the clear blue sky, the warm weather, the time with his daughter, and the buzzing thoughts of Jana. What was she thinking now? What was she feeling? Were things already moving too fast? Had he jumped ahead too many steps?

He couldn't make any promises, which meant he had to be completely honest with her. If things kept moving forward, he wouldn't mind Jana as part of his future. Heck, he'd love her to be. That thought should have scared him right out of his boots, but one could say he'd come a long way.

He'd been to hell and back, and he never wanted to return.

When a SUV pulled into the parking lot and stopped near his truck, Knox was pretty sure he stopped breathing for a handful of seconds. Then he was grinning.

Jana climbed out of the SUV, her red hair tied up into some sort of bun, her white shorts paired with a pretty red blouse, and looking like a million-and-a-half dollars.

He tried to calm down his grin as she walked to the playground, but there was no stopping it.

"Hey," she said, her gaze flitting from Knox to Ruby, who was currently on her dozenth round of going down the slide.

"Hey." He walked toward her and leaned down to kiss her cheek. She smelled sweet. Like fruit. He wanted to pull her close and kiss her for real. "How are you?"

Jana's lips twitched. "Good. And you?"

"Excellent." He winked. "Got your writing done?"

"A little."

"What's happening now between Ryan and Sandy?"

She pursed her lips, but her eyes were full of amusement. "Don't want to give out any spoilers."

Knox couldn't help it; he had to kiss her mouth. But as he leaned down, Ruby called out, "Watch, Daddy!"

Jana's brow lifted. "You're getting paged, Mr. Bull-Rider."

He kissed her on the lips before turning. "Yeah, baby?"

"Watch me fly!"

"No, Ruby." Knox sprinted to where she was getting ready to jump off one of the wide climbing ladders. The distance was only a few feet, but he wasn't taking any chances. He grasped her waist before she could move. "No jumping."

"I can do it," Ruby said. "Mom lets me."

Knox hesitated. "Well, wait for Mom, then. I want you to meet my friend."

Ruby was sufficiently distracted, and her brown eyes locked onto Jana.

"What's your name?" she asked, her tone suddenly demure.

Knox wanted to laugh. His daughter wasn't fooling anyone.

"Jana Harris," Jana said. "I saw you once in the grocery store, remember?"

Ruby scrunched up her nose. "I don't know."

Jana was smiling, though, and she extended her hand, very formal-like. But Ruby ate it up and shook Jana's hand.

"How old are you?" Ruby asked, tilting her head.

"Ruby—" Knox began.

"It's okay," Jana cut in. "I'm twenty-six. Same as your dad."

"That's a lot." Ruby wrapped her arms about Knox's neck, and he pulled her close, safely stepping away from the ladder. "I'm five."

"I thought so," Jana said. "You look like a very smart five-year-old."

Ruby grinned. "You're pretty."

Knox bit back a laugh. Leave it to Ruby to say every thought that came into her head.

"Well, thank you," Jana said. "You're pretty, too."

Ruby's shoulders sighed up and down. "Everyone tells me that."

Knox had to laugh, then, and he sure hoped Jana was taking this all with a grain of salt, even though putting any bias aside, his daughter was beautiful.

"Everyone's right," Jana said simply, her tone warm. She'd moved closer to Knox, and he liked that very much. "What's your favorite thing to do at the park?"

With no hesitation, Ruby announced, "The swings. But Daddy got tired of pushing me."

Knox groaned. "Tell her how you really feel."

"I can push you," Jana said, giving Knox a smirk as she followed Ruby to the swings.

"Can you push me really high?" Ruby said, grinning from ear to ear as she expertly hoisted herself onto the swing.

"Um..." Jana glanced at Knox. He gave a subtle shake of his head. "I think we should be listening to your dad."

Knox smiled approvingly, and Jana smiled back.

Okay, then... he should probably stop staring at her. But he was finding that his heart was soaring while he watched Jana pushing his daughter on the swing.

Ruby's laughter rang in the air, and Knox walked over to stand by Jana. He linked their fingers, and smiled when Jana's cheeks flushed pink.

"Thanks for coming," he said in a low voice. "What changed your mind?"

She looked at him with a half-smile. "You made your bed."

"What?" He chuckled. "Is that all it took? After this, I'll come clean your whole house if it gets you to hang out with me more."

Jana squeezed his hand. "Knox, you're laying it on really thick."

He leaned over and kissed her temple. "I'm glad you came. That's the truth."

"Me, too," she said.

Those two simple words were the best thing he'd heard in a long time.

"Look," Ruby was saying, "there's an airplane! Is that what you're going on tomorrow, Daddy? Mommy said you're leaving."

Knox cleared his throat. "I'm not flying on an airplane. I'm driving to San Antonio for their rodeo." He felt Jana's gaze on him, but he didn't meet her eyes. He wasn't sure where all of this was going between them, but he didn't want them to go back to not talking to each other for a bunch of years.

"In your truck that's always broken?" Ruby asked as her little legs kept pumping below her swing.

Not Over You

Knox bit back a laugh. "That same truck. She's been with me a long time."

Ruby looked back at him, which made her hair fly around her face. "Why don't you get a new one like Holt?"

Holt's truck wasn't new, but it was a heck of a lot newer than Knox's. He wanted to laugh it off, but for some reason, the comment stung a little.

Jana released his hand and slipped her arm about his waist, then whispered, "I like yours better."

He looked down at her. "You wanna go for a ride?"

Her smile only solidified his decision—and he no longer cared about his brother's newer truck.

"Let's get out of here." He must have said it too loud, because Ruby heard.

"Can we get ice cream now?"

"Sure thing," he said. He turned to Jana. "You comin'?"

Did she not realize when she bit her lip like that, it made it hard for him not to lean in and kiss her?

"I don't think so," she said. "I've got more work to do."

"Aww," Ruby said. "Don't you like ice cream?"

"I do, but I have some work." Jana then met Knox's gaze. "A little too public," she said with an apologetic smile.

Knox got it, he did. All they needed was for someone like Barb to see them together, and then everyone in Prosper would know. Which Knox wouldn't exactly mind, but he could see that Jana did. So he had to tread carefully here and respect her wishes.

As they followed Ruby to his truck, Knox asked Jana, "You coming tonight?"

"To watch you ride bulls?" she asked, the edge of her mouth quirking.

"That would be correct."

She turned to face him then. "I'll come."

His heart skipped a beat, then three. "Good." He moved a piece of hair from her face, then leaned in and kissed her.

It was much too brief, because he was interrupted by, "Daddy! I can't get the door open."

"Hang on, baby," he called to Ruby as he reluctantly stepped away from Jana. "You better not be giving me false hope, Jana Harris."

She only smiled as she walked away.

11

KNOX WON THE bull-riding event again. Jana couldn't say she was surprised, yet, it was thrilling all the same. The lights, the cheering crowd, the thundering bull—and Knox made it all look like a work of art. She'd sat by Barb and Patsy, who were never ones to miss out on any social event in Prosper that included single men. Specifically, cowboys.

"Please come to the dirt dance with us," Barb said for at least the hundredth time as the crowd filtered out of the stands.

Jana hadn't confessed to her friends about Knox staying at her place, and the turn of events in their relationship. She didn't know if she could exactly define it, anyway. He was leaving town tomorrow, and then going on to another rodeo, then another. He didn't have a permanent home that she knew of. There was still so much they hadn't even talked about.

Yet . . . when Knox had climbed up onto that bull and as he was strapping on his grip, he somehow spotted her in the stands. She'd seen his smile and had no doubt it had been just for her. Jana had never experienced such a rush of emotion before. She couldn't even fully describe it, but she still felt like she hadn't floated back to earth yet.

"You're somewhere in outer space, hon," Barb said. "Haven't you been sleeping, or something?"

"I'm fine," Jana said quickly.

"So we could go get something to eat, then come back to the dirt dance," Barb said. "What do you say, girls?"

"I'm in," Patsy announced.

But Jana was looking toward the bull-riding pen, where Knox and a couple of the other cowboys had come out to greet fans. Women surrounded them, and Jana couldn't look away from how they were obviously trying to get Knox's attention. From this distance, she couldn't see his eyes beneath his cowboy hat, and she was pretty sure he wasn't flirting back. Right?

"What are you in the mood to eat?" Barb asked Jana, cutting into her thoughts.

She exhaled and looked at her friend. "I'm not going to the dirt dance, so I'll just head home."

"Come on, Jana," Patsy said, her painted red lips forming a pout. "You've skipped out on us the last couple of times."

"Yeah, she's right," Barb cut in. Then her gaze slid to where Knox and the other bull-riders were talking to the women. "You're crushing on him, aren't you?"

"What?" Jana said. "No. I'm not crushing on anyone."

"Knox?" Patsy whispered. "Is that who we're talking about?"

Barb only nodded, her eyes wide, her brows rising in question.

"Look, I've really got to head out." Jana rose and started down the aisle. "Let me know how the dance goes."

"Jana, wait," Barb called out, while Patsy just stared at her.

"Text me," Jana said. She waved her friends off, then headed down the stands without looking back. The arena dirt was already being cleaned, and people were congregating near the walls, waiting for the dance to begin.

She wanted to talk to Knox, to plow right through those women, but she didn't want to embarrass herself, either. She'd probably end up waiting in line to talk to him. Was he going to the dirt dance? Her stomach twisted as she thought about the one from years ago, when he'd met Macie.

So it was just better that Jana leave. She was happy that Knox won again, and well, it would be amazing if things progressed with their relationship. But reality was starting to set in. Knox was currently surrounded by admiring women. So nothing had changed on that front. And what were the chances that he really would return to Prosper and want to settle down, with *her*?

She moved with the crowd leaving the arena, saying hi to a few people that she recognized. But mostly, she stayed focused on her walk back to her SUV. She hated how every approaching truck made her pulse leap in anticipation. Knox would be at the arena awhile yet.

By the time she reached her SUV, her heart felt tight, and her stomach had shrunk to the size of a pebble. She was changing her mind every few seconds. Should she stay? Congratulate Knox around all those people? Should she give him space? It wasn't like she was truly a part of his life. Yes, they'd kissed, more than once . . . But who was she to harbor expectations about him? They'd barely reconnected, and now she was falling back into old insecurities. Which, incidentally, had been partly due to Knox.

Most of all, she wondered if he'd stay for the dirt dance. He'd have plenty of women ask him to dance, there was no doubt, and Jana knew she couldn't watch it. They weren't an item, or in a relationship, at least nothing official.

So she went home. Got her laptop out, and looked up the

incoming emails that had come into the advice column to decide which one to answer. She'd focus on someone else's problems and love life. Hers had too many unknowns and variables.

Dear Miss Jewel,
My best friend is acting a lot different lately. I think he has a crush on me, and I don't know how I feel about that. I don't want to lose my best friend.
Sincerely, Unsure in Corpus Christi

Really, there were two answers. Try a relationship with the best friend, and risk losing the friendship if it didn't work out. Reject the relationship, and lose the friendship. What were the chances of a happily-ever-after in this situation if they didn't feel the same about each other?

How did Knox feel about *her*?

How did she feel about *him*?

It was too early to even know, she knew that. But it wasn't like she didn't know him. Maybe they hadn't talked for years, but she knew they were always friends first.

Jana sighed and typed a response to the email, one she'd have to fine-tune later, because she probably had too many emotions warring inside of her.

Dear Unsure in Corpus Christi,
A best friend is priceless. You need to decide how you feel first, or you will both be hurt. Look at it from his perspective. It sounds like he's willing to risk everything to have a deeper relationship with you. Are you willing to take that same risk?
Good luck.
Miss Jewel

Jana re-read her response. It was all anyone could advise without knowing more about the individuals. She closed her laptop. She didn't have the heart to answer another question for her column. What did she know about finding love and keeping relationships strong? Nothing, that's what.

She opened the document containing her novel and scrolled to the last scene. Ryan and Sandy were on their first tentative date, and as she read through the interactions of the two characters, she realized that she used dialogue that sounded like Knox. Which meant that it was easy to continue writing the scene, even though she felt like she was stealing something.

When her phone rang, it startled her out of the world she'd immersed herself in, and it took her a moment to realize that Knox was calling. She glanced at the living room clock to see it was nearly midnight. The dirt dance should be in full swing. Had he texted her, and she hadn't heard it?

Her heart was racing by the time she answered, and she was pretty sure she sounded breathless.

"Where are you?" Knox said, his voice low, but in the background, she could hear music and people.

"Home."

He said something that was muffled, to another person she guessed, then he was back on the line. "I've been looking for you, Jana. Did you ditch me?"

"Was I invited somewhere?" Maybe she shouldn't give him a hard time—after all, he'd just won the bull-riding event, so she should probably be congratulating him.

"Where'd you go?"

She pulled her legs up under her. "I told you."

"You did, but I want to know *why*." Again, he was interrupted, and she could hear someone gushing over his win.

"I didn't want to get in the way," she said. "I mean, you were surrounded by people. And I thought you'd enjoy your night more without having to worry about me."

Knox didn't say anything for a moment as the background noise shifted around him. "Remember you agreed to go for a ride in my truck?"

Of course, she remembered. "Yeah."

"How about I collect on that right now?"

She straightened. "It's really late."

He chuckled, and the sound of it was like a slow burn in her chest. "I'm not tired, are you?"

Not even close. "No," she said in an almost whisper.

"Be there in about thirty," he said. "I'll be the one in the rumbling truck pulling into your driveway."

When Jana hung up, she leapt off the couch. Knox hadn't forgotten her, not in the least. She touched up her appearance and was outside waiting for him when he pulled up to the house. She didn't want him doing anything ridiculous like honking, or even coming inside. She was worried she'd jump into his arms, and the kissing would start, and then she wouldn't be able to ask him her bigger questions.

Like what would happen once he left Prosper?

She climbed into the truck and was surprised he smelled freshly showered. He wore a dark T-shirt and faded jeans. His hat wasn't the one from the rodeo, either, but a hat that looked like the one he wore in high school. "You already cleaned up?"

He reached for her hand and pulled it onto his thigh. "I stopped in at my parents to say goodbye and cleaned up there. I'm heading to San Antonio tonight."

"You are?" She couldn't hide the surprise from her voice. Her chest was already tightening with regret. This little fling with Knox would have been better off not happening at all. She was glad to know what had split them up in high school, but reality was that they couldn't ever go back to what they used to be. Too much had happened since that time.

"Yeah, that's what I wanted to talk to you about." Knox left it at that as he continued to drive down the dark, country road. She wasn't sure where they were going until he turned on the road that led to Prosperity Ranch. This surprised her more than anything.

"Aren't your parents asleep?" she asked as they neared.

"We're not going into the house."

He parked before the road curved to the driveway, then he popped open his door, still holding her hand. "Come on," he said, tugging her so that she scooted to his side of the truck.

She stepped out, and Knox shut the driver's side door with a quiet click. Then he led her around the back side of the property, an area she knew would eventually take them past the farthest barn. She hadn't been to Prosperity Ranch for ages, since high school, really. The velvety night was warm, and the barely-there breeze raised prickles on her neck. Knox still held her hand, and she relished the warmth and strength of his fingers. She was already missing him. Wishing he didn't have to leave so soon.

"Did Ruby like the rodeo?" she finally asked, because she was truly wondering if Knox was going to say something, or if they were just walking the ranch in the middle of the night.

He seemed to come out of whatever deep thought he was in. Looking over, he pulled her to a stop. They were next to the small arena, and she assumed that in the daytime, it was filled with the horses that Holt was training and caring for. Right now, though, only silence came from the barn.

"She loved it. Asked me about a million questions, too."

"I can imagine," Jana said. "The rodeo is pretty exciting to a little girl."

"That's not what her questions were about," Knox said in

a slow tone. He lifted his hand to her neck, and his thumb did a slow caress along her jaw.

Jana involuntarily shuddered as heat pulsed through her at his touch. "What did she ask, then?"

"About you," Knox said, his tone a low murmur. "She wanted to know everything, and then she promptly told my parents that I had a girlfriend."

"What?"

His mouth quirked. "Do you want to know what I told her?"

"I don't know," Jana said. "Do I?"

Knox's hand slid lower, across her shoulder then down her arm. When his hand reached hers, he interlaced their fingers. "I told her yes."

Jana didn't know what to say. She and Knox had barely started talking to each other after years of not speaking, and—

"Jana," he said. "You don't look too happy about it."

"You told your daughter that I was your girlfriend in front of your parents? Knox, we aren't even dating, not really . . . You're leaving tonight, and then what?"

Knox brought her hand to his mouth and pressed a kiss on her knuckles. "Do we need all the answers right now?" He lifted her hand to his shoulder, then drew her hand to the back of his neck, which brought their bodies flush together.

Jana's breath stuttered. The heat between them only increased by the second. "You kissed me, Knox, and it was amazing. But it was only a kiss. Not an exclusive dating commitment."

"Hmm," his voice rumbled. "Are you a player, Jana Harris?"

She wanted to laugh, but his tone had been completely serious. "No. I'm not a player, but . . ."

He leaned his forehead against hers. "You don't trust me, do you?"

Jana closed her eyes. "I do trust you. Or at least, I want to."

Knox's exhale was slow. "I guess I deserve that. I'm sure you've heard all the rumors. Most of them are probably true. But I want you to know that you can ask me anything, sweetheart, anything at all."

"I'm at a disadvantage here," she said, opening her eyes.

"How so?"

"You're Knox Prosper," she said. "Every woman in the town has been in love with you at one point or another. But I'm just plain Jana. I make jam for my parents' tiny company. I write novels that no one wants to buy. I've been on maybe ten dates since high school. Believe me, no one is lining up to date me. No one even cares enough to gossip about me. Unless it's connected with you, of course."

Knox lifted his other hand and ran it behind her head, into her hair. Goose bumps skittered across her skin at his touch, his nearness. "You're not just any woman, Jana. That's why I brought you here before I have to take off again."

"You keep saying that," she said. "What are you talking about?"

"Look," he said, turning so that they were both facing the ranch house, even though it was at a distance. The summer moon made the white ranch house silvery, and the shapes and shadows of the barn, the arena, and the tended lawn were like a postcard.

"This is what I want," he said in a soft voice. "And I want to know what you think about it."

"You want Prosperity Ranch?"

"No." He slipped his arm across her shoulders while they stood side by side. "I want my own place. My own ranch.

Where my wife can raise our babies and make as much jam as she wants. Or write a book."

"Knox," Jana whispered. "I can't believe you're saying all of this. You can't possibly know that we're . . . going to be like that."

"I don't know one hundred percent." He pulled her closer. "Because you'd have to be a part of that percent."

She turned toward him in the crook of his arm. His mouth was only inches away, and she could swear she heard his heartbeat. Racing as fast as hers. "Knox . . ."

"Come to San Antonio," he whispered. "Hang out with me. We can begin to figure out what's going on between us. Slowly. Like it should be." Before she could fully comprehend what he was suggesting, he dipped his head and brushed his lips against hers. Ever so gently.

Jana couldn't have defined what it felt like being this close to Knox, her body nestled against his, as the night deepened and cooled around them. "Going to San Antonio to watch you in the rodeo feels like chasing you."

"You can't chase something that's not running." His lips strayed to her jawline, and he pressed his mouth there.

Jana's skin pebbled at his touch, and she was done with the teasing, light kisses. She wanted more of this man. She grasped his shirt and tugged him closer with a determination that surprised even her.

Knox's mouth lifted into a smile before he claimed her mouth. The heat built instantly, and he hoisted her close. Her fingers trailed behind his warm neck, then into his hair as she clung to him. Knox's hands moved along her back as he angled his mouth over hers for a deeper kiss.

Everything about this night, about this kiss, about his sweet words, would have made any woman swoon. Except Jana had spent years trying to get over this man . . . none of it had worked. She'd had her heart broken once, and letting him in again would only set her up for a heartbreak she didn't know if she could recover from.

"Knox," she whispered, drawing away. "This feels too good to be true."

Knox gazed at her through half-closed eyes, sending another round of heat through her. "I agree. I don't deserve you, but I want to try to be worthy of you, of this, of us having a second chance."

Jana's eyes pricked with tears—why, she couldn't define it. Knox was saying things beyond her wildest hopes. Could she trust in it? In him? Could she let go of the images of those women flocking to him, knowing that he hadn't always turned down those types of women? And that had been the issue that had ended his marriage.

Knox's baggage was heavy. Was she strong enough to help him carry it?

12

ON THE WALK back to the truck with Jana, Knox had seen a light peeking through the barn door. That meant the light had either been left on, or someone was in the office. When he saw Holt's truck in his parents' driveway, Knox's heart sank. Why was Holt here in the middle of the night? Was something wrong?

He didn't bring it up to Jana. He was fighting enough battles with her—primarily to get her to come to San Antonio. There, he believed, they could go out, spend time together while not surrounded by everything that reminded them of their shared past. And *his* past that ultimately drove them apart and prevented any reconciliation.

He wanted to make new memories with her, fresh ones. He hated that she'd hesitated more than once tonight. Yet, it told him she was thinking about their relationship, deeply. This was a good thing in the long run, he decided. He wasn't planning on letting Jana go anytime soon. He just had to prove his true intentions and prove that his old life was completely over. Dead. Gone.

"Here we are," Jana said as he stopped in front of her house. A couple of lights were on inside, and the house looked cozy and cheerful. Like a place he could feel welcomed and comfortable.

"Here we are," Knox repeated, looking over at Jana's profile.

She sold herself short—she always had. Her comment about being "plain Jana" was so far from the truth that he'd almost laughed. But he'd known she was serious, and whatever her insecurities were, he hoped to completely erase them.

"Call me tomorrow morning?" he said, just to see her reaction, because he definitely planned on calling her. A lot. And texting. Until he saw her again.

Her gaze shifted to his, and her pretty mouth curved. "Won't you be sleeping in?"

"No," he said. "I've got to check into the arena early for my practice time. And then I'll be wondering when you're coming up."

"I can't just drop everything."

"Is there pickup on Sunday?"

"No..."

Knox grinned. "See, perfect. I'll book you a room, and you can stay the night, then drive back Monday morning."

Jana shook her head, but she was smiling. "Knox..."

He leaned over and kissed her, lingering, breathing her in. He couldn't believe how hard it was to say goodbye to her right now. When he couldn't find her after the rodeo, he'd been truly worried—wondering if she'd blown him off. If things were over before they'd really started. But then she'd agreed to go for a ride, and he knew that there was no turning back—at least for his heart.

Being around Jana felt comfortable. He felt like he could be his true self. Not that guy who everyone looked up to for being a rodeo star, and not the guy who everyone in his family looked down on for screwing up things with Macie.

Yet, Jana had misgivings. That was as plain as day.

"Knox, I should go," she said, still close enough to kiss. "Drive safe and good luck tomorrow night."

He grasped her waist before she could pull away. "Is that it? Good luck?" he teased.

She smiled and rested her hand on his jaw. "Things are complicated."

"They'll always be complicated," he said. "But let's do complicated together." He stole another kiss, or two.

Until she sighed and pulled away. "Tempting."

"Is that a yes?"

Jana smirked. "It's a *good luck tomorrow*."

Knox groaned, but then he walked her to the front porch. Hugged her, stole more kisses, then walked away feeling like he was both walking on water, and dragging an anchor behind him. He was gratified, though, when Jana remained in the doorway until he pulled out of the driveway. He'd start heading to San Antonio soon enough, but first, he wanted to see if Holt was still at the ranch.

When he pulled up to the ranch, the glimmer of light from the barn was still visible.

Knox hoped whatever was going on, it would be fixable. Did Holt often work in the office in the middle of the night, or was something wrong?

He knocked on the barn door before opening it, even though the office was its own interior room. But Holt had heard him and was at the office doorway by the time Knox walked in.

His brother wore no cowboy hat and looked as if he'd been scrubbing a hand through his brown hair. His shirt was rumpled, rolled up at the sleeves, and open at the collar. His blue gaze tracked Knox as he crossed to him.

"Is everything okay?" Knox asked. "I saw your truck and the light in here."

Holt rubbed a hand over his face, then scuffed his boot across the ground. "Come in. We need to talk, anyway."

Knox tried to ignore the pinch in his gut. "You get the money I transferred yesterday?"

"Yep. Sure did. Thanks for that."

Knox felt only slightly mollified. He still owed a few thousand more to Holt, and Knox intended to make good on every red cent of it.

Holt nodded to the extra chair in the office, and Knox took it. He had no idea what to expect from his brother, and frankly, it wasn't so pleasant being in such close quarters with him. They'd had plenty of disagreements, and even an outright fistfight last summer when Knox had accused Holt of stealing Macie. Which had ended up being true, but then again, Macie was no longer Knox's wife to be stolen.

"Look at this," Holt said, turning the glowing computer screen so that Knox could see an email that had been pulled up.

It was from the horse rehabilitation grant division, and as Knox read through it, he realized that the grant that Holt had depended on to rehabilitate sick, neglected, or injured horses was being cut in half. "Who the heck is RD & Associates?"

"Another outfit that's applied for funding in our same town," Holt said. "Which means that our funds will be cut significantly, since the organization is promising to bring in a volunteer veterinarian to work with the more difficult cases. The vet care bills will be virtually nonexistent. The writing's on the wall. We could easily lose the grant altogether since this other place could rehabilitate more horses at less cost. This would look attractive to the board of directors."

Not Over You

Knox heard the restraint in Holt's voice. His brother was truly upset, but like all things, he was managing his emotions about the huge setback. "Who are these yahoos?"

"I haven't gotten that far," Holt said. "I saw the email come in on my phone during the rodeo, but didn't want to worry anyone. Couldn't sleep, so I headed over here to hopefully get my head around this."

Knox pulled out his phone and googled the name of the organization listed in the letter, then clicked the tab with the board of directors listed. "Well, I'll be . . ."

"What?" Holt asked.

Knox could hardly believe it himself. "Judd Harris is on the board of directors. What are the chances that he directed RD & Associates to set up in Prosper? Give you a little competition, or something?"

Holt frowned. "Judd? He doesn't even live in Prosper anymore. Gave their daughter the operations part of the business, then they hightailed it out of here."

"San Antonio is where they ended up," Knox said. His mind was reeling. He'd known Judd Harris his whole life—everyone in Prosper did. But Knox hadn't had much interaction with the man. Yeah, Knox had dated Jana, but he'd not spent much time at her house or around her parents during those months.

He felt his brother's gaze on him, and Knox looked up. At the steely look in Holt's blue eyes, Knox said, "What?"

"Ruby said something about Jana being your girlfriend?" The hard line of Holt's jaw flexed.

"Ruby's interpretation is a little different than reality," Knox said, frowning. "We're dating, I guess, but things are pretty fresh."

Holt gave a short nod. "You kept in touch with her all these years?"

Knox squared his shoulders. "No, of course not. Why would you say that? I was married to Macie."

Holt folded his arms. "That didn't stop you—"

Knox leapt to his feet, and Holt did, too. Holt was taller than Knox, but Knox was just as strong. "Stop bringing up the past," Knox ground out, proud of himself for not already having hit his brother. "Nothing good will come of it."

Holt's gaze dropped a fraction, then he lifted it again to focus on Knox. "You're right. But answer me one thing straight up."

Knox dipped his chin. "Of course."

"Did you give Jana or her dad information about the grant?"

Knox clenched his jaw for a good three seconds. How could his brother even *think* that would happen? Yet, the steady blue of Holt's eyes told Knox that his brother didn't want to believe it, but it was a necessary question.

"Listen," Knox said, his tone low, barely controlled. "First, I never spoke to or saw Jana Harris until this week. The last time I saw her was at the rodeo where I . . . we . . . met Macie." He exhaled. "Second, this might come as a shock to you, but Jana and I haven't discussed you or your job here once. I know you think everyone in Prosper is always talking about our family, but we weren't. Besides, this offer didn't happen overnight. I'm assuming it's been in the works for months. You said yourself it took several weeks to get your approvals."

Holt nodded at this.

"The timing doesn't line up," Knox said. "I've only been hanging out with Jana for a few days, and well, I can't vouch for Judd Harris's decisions, but I'd never undercut our parents' ranch. Never. Even if you and I hated each other, I'd still honor our parents."

"I don't hate you," Holt said in a quiet voice. His blue eyes had lost their steel.

Knox rubbed a hand over his face. When it all came down to it, he didn't hate his brother, either. "Good to know."

The edge of Holt's mouth lifted. "Now, let's figure this out. If you didn't tell Jana, and she never brought it up, do you think she knows?"

Knox returned to his seat. "I don't know. She seems pretty busy, and well . . ." His voice trailed off. Was Jana's reluctance to date him tied to the fact that her father was undercutting his brother?

No . . . But the question wouldn't leave his mind. Even if Jana knew about it, what did that mean? She might not even understand the full scope of the issue this brought to Prosperity Ranch. The grant had quite literally saved the ranch from having to sell off pieces of property.

"I'm going to make calls on Monday morning," Holt said. "Maybe it's not as grim as it looks, but I'm not holding out much hope. Unless we can magically find a volunteer vet."

Knox scoffed. "That doesn't make sense. What vet would do such a thing? Unless he had some other incentive going?"

Holt puffed out a breath. "I don't know. You got me there. Maybe Lane will know which direction we can go."

Knox didn't miss the "we" in Holt's statement. Was his brother finally including him in something to do with the ranch? Yeah, Knox had blown his portion, but he wanted to pay back everything he'd borrowed from his brother, then begin the process of investing. If he kept winning bull-riding events and living frugally, he'd eventually get there. "Let me talk to Jana, see what she knows," he said. "Maybe I can even talk to Judd Harris."

Holt's brows raised. "Could you? I mean, I have no problem calling up Judd Harris, but the conversation isn't going to be friendly."

"And we can probably catch more flies with honey," Knox said.

"That's right." Holt leaned back in his chair, the lines about his eyes relaxing. "Thanks, man. Maybe it can be salvaged after all. I don't know how, but it's better than doing nothing."

Knox nodded. "No problem."

Silence fell between the two brothers. When Holt finally spoke up, he said, "Look, I'm sorry about accusing you. I'm just frustrated. I can see you've worked really hard at some personal stuff. It's obvious to all of us—the whole family."

"Thanks," Knox said in a quiet voice.

"Ruby thinks you walk on water, you know," Holt said, a half-smile on his face.

"Yeah, I don't know if I can ever live up to who she thinks I am." Knox rubbed his palms over his knees. "When she looks at me like I'm her world, I don't know whether to be proud, or discouraged."

Holt gazed at him for a second, then lowered his eyes. "I think we've all had a lot to learn as a family, and hopefully, things will only get better from here."

"I hope so, too."

Holt's smile appeared. "Hey, maybe you'll be the one to save the ranch after all."

Knox chuckled. "That'll be the day. Don't let anyone hold their breath." He rose to his feet, and Holt rose, too.

This time, instead of almost getting into a fistfight, they shook hands.

"Keep me posted," Holt said.

"Will do." Knox released his hand and turned to go.

Before Knox reached the outer barn door, Holt said, "Good luck with Jana, too. Despite all this stuff, I'm glad you're seeing her."

Not Over You

Knox looked over at his brother with surprise. "Really?"

Holt lifted a shoulder. "Yeah. I always wondered why you guys didn't stay together."

Knox nodded. "It's complicated. But we talked through a few things, so . . ." He didn't finish, because he didn't really know how to define their relationship. If Jana didn't come to San Antonio, then he wasn't sure when he'd see her again.

"Good luck at tomorrow's rodeo," Holt said.

Knox left then. His mind pulled in different directions. The rodeo in San Antonio was the least of his concerns. He'd hate to see his family's ranch put in financial straits again. And what was the deal with Judd Harris and RD & Associates? Did Jana know anything about the boards her father sat on?

Knox didn't want to believe she did, but how could he really be one hundred percent sure? How well did he really know Jana? All of their interactions had been mostly flirtatious. By the time he climbed back into his truck and was on the road to San Antonio, he was wondering if he'd imagined the closeness he'd felt with Jana. Perhaps, it was just old memories that had resurfaced. The desire to go back in time, to a period in his life that held way fewer complications.

Just an hour ago, he was sure he was falling in love with her. But now . . . He groaned inwardly, hating how fickle his emotions were being.

If it wasn't so late, he'd call her right now. Ask her point blank.

He probably wasn't in the best frame of mind to do so. The last thing he wanted was to make Jana feel like he was coming down on her. Drumming his fingers against the steering wheel, he thought about it from all angles. What if the worst-case scenario happened, and Prosperity Ranch had their grant funds cut? What else could bring in additional income?

Knox thought through the aspects of the ranch. Holt had

been training rodeo horses from all over the state before the grant. But as small-town rodeos had been dying out for the last decade, those clients had faded. The ranch's clientele had been drastically reduced. So Holt had started traveling around the state, and even to ranches out of state, to train rodeo horses. But that took him away from the ranch management, and with their parents getting older, someone else needed to step in.

But Knox was off following his dreams, and Lane was in school.

Now, Knox hoped he could help in some way to keep Prosperity Ranch running to its full potential. If the grant thing couldn't be changed, then he'd have to come up with something to help.

By mid-morning the next day, Knox hadn't slept more than a few hours, and he'd already done his practice round through the San Antonio arena. Jana hadn't called, which he had to admit, he felt a little disappointed in. But he wasn't going to let that stop him from calling her.

He hung up his rodeo gear in his assigned space, then walked out into the arena, where some other cowboys were going through some practice drills. He pulled out his cell phone and called Jana's number. It rang three times, then went to voicemail. Was that early? Had she blocked his call?

He turned his focus to the cowboy swinging his rope, missing the calf by about a foot. Roping had never been his thing, but hats off to the cowboys who did it. Five minutes passed, maybe ten. Who was counting? He dialed Jana again.

This time, she answered. "Hello?"

Relief flooded through him immediately, and he knew all the doubtful feelings he'd built up over the drive to San Antonio and throughout this morning had disappeared in an instant. He was just happy to hear her voice, happy that she'd answered.

"You didn't call."

"No *how are you doing*, or *thanks for answering my call?*"

Knox smiled at the teasing tone in her voice. "How are you, sweetheart? And thank you from the bottom of my heart for answering your phone."

Jana laughed. But it wasn't through the phone. It was . . .

He turned to see a beautiful sight.

Jana was walking toward him. She was *here*. Really here. His gaze soaked in all of her. From the red waves about her shoulders, to the white blouse, to her black jeans and black boots. She looked classy and elegant. And his heart had completely melted.

"Are you a mirage?" he said, unable to stop the grin on his face.

Her smile was absolutely breathtaking. "Judge for yourself, Mr. Bull-Rider."

He wasn't wasting another second; he strode to her, then scooped her into his arms. Lifting her, he spun her slowly.

"Knox, put me down," Jana said with a laugh.

He obliged, but he didn't release her. Frankly, he never wanted to release her. Jana in his arms felt like heaven had come down to earth. "You're not a mirage," he whispered.

"I'm not," she whispered back.

He closed the distance between them, his mouth finding hers. She grasped his shoulders as he kissed her. He pushed away any questions he had about her dad's business, and just breathed in everything about her—her sweet scent, the warmth of her mouth, the press of her body against his.

"Knox," Jana murmured. "We're in public."

"I know," he murmured back, then kept kissing her, his hands shifting to cradle her face.

"You need to cool it off." Her tone held amusement.

"I know," he murmured again, his mouth moving to her jaw.

"Right now."

Knox buried his face against her neck. He exhaled, and Jana slid her hands down his arms. She stepped away from him, and he lifted his head, feeling like he'd just awakened from a deep, delicious dream.

Jana was watching him, her eyes dancing. "Did you miss me?"

He grasped her hand. "You have no idea."

She looked down at their interlocked fingers as his thumb stroked over her wrist. "I missed you, too."

"Did I hear you right? Did you just admit you like me, Jana Harris?"

Jana nudged him. "Don't tease me."

"What if I like teasing you?"

Her gaze clung to his, and his stomach bottomed out because he felt himself falling. In love. It was physical, emotional, and all-encompassing. Could she see it in his eyes? Had he just given himself away, and now, she'd be scared off?

"How'd your practice go?" she asked.

It took him a second to come out of the fog his mind had entered. "Great. Everything's looking good. I had a chance to chat with Running Hot. We're gonna get along just fine."

Jana laughed.

He loved her laughter.

"Is that so? You had a conversation with a bull?"

"Yes, ma'am."

She smirked, and he leaned down and kissed her nose. Her hand strayed to his chest, and it was doubly hard to pull away.

"So . . . you want to get some lunch?" he said.

"You never give up, do you?"

Knox chuckled. "You came all this way. I'm figuring a man can presume."

This time, she rose up on her toes and kissed his cheek. He knew he'd feel that imprint for a long time.

"All right, let's go to lunch," she said. "You buying?"

"Always."

She grinned, and her fingers tightened in his. Knox couldn't deny it—his heart was soaring. They headed toward the arena exit and found his truck in the parking lot. He kept ahold of her hand as they walked to the driver's side of the truck.

"Oh, so we're getting in your truck cowboy style?" Jana quipped as she climbed in on his side. She sat in the middle of the bench.

"Yes, ma'am," he said. "That way, you don't get too far from me."

"What are we, seventeen again?"

"No, thank goodness," he said, settling beside her, then starting the truck. "I don't like all those silent years between us."

Jana merely grasped his hand when it was free, saying nothing.

When they arrived at a small Tex Mex restaurant, Knox said, "By the way, my sister Evie is coming tonight. Probably with her boyfriend, Carson Hunt."

"Oh, okay."

"You can sit with them if you want," Knox continued. "If you're okay with that?"

Jana shrugged, not seeming too enthused.

Knox pulled into a parking space, then shut off the engine. Facing Jana, he said, "What?"

She gave him a smile that didn't exactly reach her eyes. "It's just . . . your family."

"And?"

She bit her lip, which only notched up his pulse.

"I told my parents you're my girlfriend—even though you already disputed that. But in my book, we're dating. What about your book?"

Jana sighed, and Knox wasn't sure that was a good sign. But she'd come all this way—didn't that mean something?

"I don't know, Knox," she said, regret in her tone. "It feels like pressure. I mean, I know Evie, of course. But now she'll know—which means your whole family will know—that I came here for you. And there will be questions, and speculations, and—"

Knox placed a finger over her lips. "Hush, sweetheart. I'll tell my sister absolutely no questions allowed. I don't think you'll have trouble with Carson—he's a quiet guy—but I can warn him as well."

Jana rolled her eyes. "I'm being serious."

"I am, too," Knox said, leaning close and brushing his mouth against hers. "If you don't want to sit by them, no problem. But I'm pretty sure they're going to know you're at the rodeo. I'm not that good at hiding my intentions."

Jana tilted her head and skimmed her fingers over the scruff of his jaw. "And what are your intentions, sir?"

"To convince you that I've got my eyes only on you."

Her smile was slow, even shy. "You're doing a decent job so far."

He chuckled. "Good to hear. Come on. Let's eat. I don't want you to waste away."

"I'm guessing you're hungry," she said.

"Starving."

13

IT TURNED OUT that Knox was one persuasive guy—or charming or just plain flattering—because Jana was currently sitting next to his sister Evie and her boyfriend, Carson Hunt. Evie was dressed like she was going to a corporate dinner, her blonde hair pulled up into a tight twist, further accenting her pretty blue eyes. Whereas Carson looked like he fit in with every cowboy in the arena. He wore a cowboy hat over his dark hair, and his nearly black eyes were currently focused on the calf-roping in the arena. He hadn't let go of Evie's hand once, and it was clear that Carson adored her, and she adored him right back.

Jana might be a tad envious of that new, unweighted love, one with no traumatic history.

Whereas she and Knox . . . things were complicated from the get-go.

Jana couldn't help but glance at Evie with her boyfriend. She was happy for the pair. Evie had been really quiet in school, and they'd never exactly been friends. Barb was friends with everyone, and so that had been Jana's bridge to Evie. Besides, Jana had always sensed that Evie didn't like her dating her brother way back then.

What did she think now? Maybe this could be a fresh start, or was Evie just pretending to be nice right now?

Barb would probably laugh at the situation that Jana now found herself in. But she hadn't told anyone she'd come up today. Not even her parents, who lived only a few miles from the arena. If she got the orders filled on Monday, what did it matter to anyone? Yet, Jana knew exactly why she hadn't told anyone about this little trip. It was because she didn't know how to define it. Despite all of Knox's charm and sweet, flattering words, she was going into this with her eyes wide open. Whatever *this* was.

"Wanna load up on snacks?" Evie said, fiddling with her earring as she looked over at Jana.

It was the second time Evie had asked, as if she wanted to escape the rodeo events for a bit. Obviously, she wasn't as enthralled with what was going on as Carson.

"Okay," Jana conceded, even though she wasn't hungry. She'd eaten her fill at lunch with Knox, and she still felt like she might burst out of her jeans.

"Great." Evie flashed her a smile, then turned to Carson. "We're getting some food. Be right back, babe."

He pulled her close and whispered something in her ear. Jana hid a smile when Evie's neck flushed. Then he drew away and pulled out his wallet.

"No, I've got it," Evie said, pushing Carson's wallet away. Then she stood and motioned for Jana to follow.

Jana nodded goodbye to Carson, who soon turned his attention to the arena again. The bull-riding was still a ways off, since it was usually reserved as the last event of the night.

Once she and Evie reached the portal, Evie said, "We need to talk."

Jana's brows lifted. Was getting snacks a ruse? "Okay,"

she said easily, even though her stomach had instantly knotted.

Evie tilted her head for Jana to follow her to a quiet spot between a shop area selling souvenirs, and one of the concessions counters. When Evie stopped and turned around, she folded her arms, her blue eyes anything but friendly.

Jana braced herself for whatever Evie might throw at her. Apparently, the woman wasn't happy after all with Jana dating her brother.

"Did you get pregnant in high school?" Evie asked.

Jana's mouth nearly dropped open. "What? No. I mean . . ." She swallowed. How far had that rumor gone? "I took a pregnancy test, but it was negative. Soon after, Knox and I broke up, anyway." Why were her eyes stinging with tears? Just talking about this reminded her of the emotions she'd faced, and now, being confronted by one of Knox's sisters was like adding salt to the wound.

Evie studied her for a moment, and Jana held the woman's gaze. She was telling the truth, and everyone would just have to accept it. But now, Jana wondered . . . "Did you tell people I was? Did *you* spread the rumor?"

Evie blinked and stepped back. "No. I wouldn't do something like that. Especially if I thought it would hurt my brother, as annoying and stubborn as he could be back then."

Jana had to believe her. She had no other choice. "I'm sorry you thought I hid something like that. I said something to one of my friends that must have been overheard by the wrong person."

"Yeah, I get it." Evie touched one of her earrings again. "Small towns and all. I'm not sad to be out of Prosper for good."

This surprised Jana, because she heard real disdain in

Evie's voice. "You're not loyal to Prosper through and through?"

Evie looked away for a moment, then said, "I'm loyal to my family, sure, but not the town. Although, Carson is trying to break down my defenses."

Ah. That made sense. "Because of his grandpa living there?" Carson Hunt's grandpa had retired to Prosper, and he'd invested money into fixing up the rodeo arena, as well as built some stables on his property to help Holt Prosper with overflow for his rehabilitating horses.

"Yeah, and the high school tried to hire me," Evie said in a slow voice, still not meeting Jana's eyes. "I went in there for an interview. But . . . that place has some rough memories."

Suddenly, Evie's gaze was on Jana, hard and penetrating. "I'm sure for you, high school was a dream. Especially since you could get away with bullying others."

Jana blinked, then frowned. "Excuse me?"

Evie set her hands on her hips. "Don't pretend you don't know what I'm talking about. You filled my locker with garbage, and you tripped me that one time in front of everyone."

Jana felt her face drain of all warmth, then heat back up. "I . . ." She closed her eyes. High school was so long ago, and her vivid memories all centered on Knox. But filling Evie's locker with garbage? She snapped her eyes open. "Look, I never put garbage in your locker. I promise. I don't know who told you that, but—"

"No one told me," Evie said. "It happened the day after you tripped me, and the whole school laughed at me, including Douglas. I'd heard he was going to ask me to prom. But the next thing I knew, my locker had been filled with garbage, and Douglas asked *you* to prom. To top it all off,

Not Over You

you'd broken my brother's heart." Tears spilled down Evie's cheeks, and she wiped at them furiously.

Now, Jana's mouth fell open. "Oh my gosh, Evie," she said, her own heart feeling like it was ripping. "I didn't know that . . . I . . . Yeah, I tripped you, and it was dumb. Really dumb. Douglas dared me to trip the next person to come out of Mr. Gardner's class. You were it. But I swear . . . I *swear* I didn't put garbage in your locker."

Evie didn't answer, but continued to wipe at her tears.

Jana dug out some tissue from her bag and handed it over. "*Please* forgive me for tripping you. I should have apologized later, and I wanted to, but the thing between Knox and I had my emotions all tied into knots. I should have never gone to prom with Douglas, anyway. We fought the whole time after he accused me of still liking Knox."

Evie sniffled and wadded up the tissue in her hand, not meeting Jana's eyes.

"Please, you have to know how sorry I am," Jana said. "I shouldn't have tripped anyone. And I'm sorry about your locker. If you find out who it was, I'll go break some kneecaps."

Evie peeked at Jana. "You're not just saying that because you want my approval for you to date my brother again?"

Jana exhaled. "Look. Knox and I are . . . I don't know, hanging out? We got some things straightened out between us, and I guess we're sort of dating now. Not officially, though. I mean, I'm still trying to figure out where he is in his life, and where I am in relation to it."

"Knox said you were his girlfriend."

Jana's cheeks heated up. "Yeah, I heard."

Evie looked surprised at this. "So it's not a two-way street."

It was Jana's turn to look away. "I won't deny that Knox

has always had part of my heart, and always will. But I'm not seventeen anymore. And I know things have been complicated in his life."

Evie laughed, and Jana looked at her in surprise.

"That about sums it up," Evie said, still smiling. "I for one am glad you aren't blinded by Knox's way with the ladies."

Jana nodded. "Honestly, that's what worries me most." There, it was out there. In actual conversation. To Knox's own sister.

Evie moved closer and put a hand on Jana's arm. "Look, Knox's past mistakes aren't any of my business. But I know he's paid a lot of penance. He's changed. Everyone in our family can see that. Losing Macie, and almost losing Ruby, really shook him up."

Jana exhaled, then nodded. "I know he's changed . . . but it's hard for me to trust in good things sometimes."

"I get that more than probably everyone." Evie smiled, her tears completely gone now. "Want my advice?"

"Of course," Jana said. "I could definitely use any advice now."

"Take it one day at a time."

The advice was simple—so simple that Jana should have thought of it. "Okay, I will."

"Oh, and Jana," Evie said, "I've never seen Knox like this around another woman. Not even his ex-wife when they were first together. So for what it's worth, to him, you are the real deal."

Jana was speechless.

"Now," Evie continued, "let's get those snacks."

Jana followed her to the concessions, feeling like she'd just lived through two lifetimes. Things between her and Evie were cleared up, and things with her and Knox? More promising than she expected.

Not Over You

"Let me help you carry that stuff," Jana said as Evie began to scoop up her purchases. "Hungry?"

Evie laughed. "It's for all of us."

Once they joined Carson back in the arena, the bull-riding was announced. Evie settled next to Carson, grasping his hand. Jana watched each bull-rider, paying more attention than she ever had to the sport, now that she understood it better.

When Knox's name was called, Evie and Carson jumped to their feet to cheer. Jana joined them, her heart thudding, almost in time to her clapping. They took their seats, but Jana's heart was still in the air, jumping each time the bull bucked and tried to throw off its rider.

"I don't know why he beats himself up like that," Evie said, gripping Jana's hand as the announcer counted down the time.

When the buzzer rang, everyone cheered. His ride had been great, but there had been a couple of other great ones, too. Would Knox be able to pull it off?

Evie started eating the nachos like she was starving. "I'm a stress eater," she said, then ate another chip.

Jana would have laughed, but her heart was in her throat. Finally, the announcer said that Knox had won by a single point. She jumped to her feet, cheering as loud as she could.

The winners of the rodeo events were paraded back into the arena, and the awards were handed over. "Let's go congratulate him," Evie said.

"Right on the arena floor?" Jana asked, following the pair as they headed to the aisle.

Evie glanced back. "Sure, why not?"

Why not? Because Knox was surrounded, and Jana would rather hang back. Wait until he was alone—which she realized now would probably never happen while he was still in the arena.

Evie and Carson seemed to have no problem making their way through the crowd, so Jana kept close behind them. Still, when they reached the group surrounding Knox, Jana's stomach took a nosedive. Most of the people simply shook his hand, and a few asked for pictures. Some of the women were making their interest clear, though.

Evie scoffed as they overheard one woman ask for his number.

"Write it on my arm, darlin'," said a woman with brows so thick, they must've been painted on.

"Sorry, sugar, my girlfriend wouldn't be happy." Then he looked over at Jana and winked.

She didn't even realize he knew she was at the back of the crowd.

The eyebrow woman turned and stared at Jana.

What in the world . . . ? Jana felt her cheeks heat, but she refused to look away from the woman who had no business asking Knox for his number in the first place. Single or not. In that moment, Jana saw another side of Knox's life. Where he had to turn down pestering people who only looked at him for his outer fame, and didn't care about anything beyond that.

The eyebrow woman turned back to Knox. "I can still give you my number, just in case."

Knox chuckled. "Have a great evening, and thanks for coming." Then he turned to the next person, a woman with her son, and signed a poster for them.

Jana didn't even know there were posters of Knox. Wow. Pretty amazing. Evie and Carson shuffled forward, waiting their turn, and Jana moved with them. She felt detached from those pressing for a moment of Knox's time, and she looked at these people from another perspective. They were here as fans, nothing else. Except for that eyebrow woman—and there were probably more like her.

But Knox wasn't responsible for another person's behavior. He was only responsible for his own. He was handling these people remarkably well, with friendliness and professionalism. His personality was naturally charming, but he wasn't crossing any lines. Not now, and not at the rodeo in Prosper, Jana realized.

Evie had said her brother had changed from the issues he'd had with Macie, and Jana was now a current witness to it. Somehow, she knew that even if she hadn't come tonight, Knox would still be putting off the woman. Not for her, specifically, but because of his own decisions.

Jana moved forward again. Finally, the crowd had thinned, and about half the people he'd greeted and taken pictures with were now gone.

"Congrats, bro," Evie said, stepping forward to hug him.

Knox grinned and hugged her tight, then he released her and clasped hands with Carson.

"You were amazing," Carson said. "I think you get better every time I see you."

"Thanks, man," Knox said, his green eyes shifting to Jana.

"Congratulations," she said as someone jostled her from behind. She nearly tripped forward, but Knox grasped her.

"Sorry," she said. "Your fans are pretty wild."

Knox grinned and pulled her closer. "What about you?"

Her heart was already hammering, and now, he was going to make her blush in front of everyone?

"Selfie, everyone!" Evie announced, moving to the other side of Knox. She held up her phone as Carson crowded behind them.

Knox's arm snaked around Jana's waist more fully, and just before Evie took the picture, he kissed Jana's cheek.

"Hey, look at the camera, Knox," Evie said with a laugh.

Knox did, grinning, and Jana wanted to laugh with giddiness. She herself was turning into quite the fan of Knox Prosper. Evie and Carson stepped away, but Knox didn't release Jana.

"Dinner after?" he said to his sister and her boyfriend.

"Of course," Evie said. "Where should we meet?"

"I'll text you when we decide," Knox said, apparently including Jana in the "we."

He still hadn't released her, and when she made a move to step away and give him space with the waiting fans, he grasped her hand.

"Where are you going?" he asked, his gaze fully focused on her like there weren't twenty people waiting for autographs and pictures.

"I can wait by your truck."

"Wait with me," he said. "These folks are friendly."

She was totally blushing now, and she really didn't want to argue with him in front of all these waiting people. "Okay."

Knox smiled, then leaned down and kissed her on the mouth.

She was so shocked, she didn't move. He only smiled, then turned to the next person waiting to talk to him. When pictures were requested, he released her hand and obliged, but through it all, he managed to continue holding her hand most of the time. He even stole another kiss, and Jana wondered how many photos there were out there now of them kissing.

She knew she'd feel more self-conscious later about it all, but right now, she felt like she was existing in a dream state. Was this all truly real? Knox's pointed attention on her when so many others were vying for his?

When the line finally dwindled to the last person, Knox sent the young man off with a selfie of the two of them and a signed program. Then he turned to Jana and slipped his hands about her waist. She rested her hands on his biceps, feeling the warm heat beneath the cotton of his shirt. The green of his eyes was solely focused on her, and he smelled of dirt and spice and man. She wanted everyone and everything to disappear so she could kiss him properly.

"Thanks for waiting with me," he said in a low voice. The arena had mostly cleared out, but there were still plenty of people around.

"I could have just waited in the parking lot," she said.

"You told me that," he said, his gaze straying to her mouth, then lower. "You look beautiful."

For an instant, Jana couldn't even remember which outfit she'd chosen that night. Knox's intense gaze was crowding out all of her short-term memory. "You look like you just won a rodeo."

He chuckled, then pulled her closer.

Before she knew it, his mouth was on hers, and the scruff along his jaw was scraping her skin as he deepened his kiss.

Well, then . . .

Knox had no trouble with PDA, it seemed. Jana curled her fingers into his shirt to keep herself in balance. So, this dating Knox thing was pretty much a different universe to exist in.

"Let's get out of here," he whispered.

14

KNOX WAS IN a good mood. A very good mood. His sister had warmed to Jana, and to be honest, he'd been worried about that. Not that Evie's disapproval would have changed his mind about Jana. But having family support was always nice, especially since he'd cut himself off from it for so long.

But on the drive over to the restaurant, Jana had told him about her conversation with his sister, how they'd worked things out. And that was just peachy with Knox.

Now, as they all sat at a restaurant, he smiled as Jana and Evie swapped stories about growing up in Prosper. And Barb. Ah, Barb was always the center of attention wherever she went.

"Next time you're in Prosper, you should hang out with us," Jana told his sister.

Evie looked surprised, but pleased. She reached for Carson's hand, then said, "Maybe I will."

Jana smiled. "Good to hear. What's your cell number?"

The women swapped numbers, and Knox hoped it meant they would officially be friends. He draped an arm across the back of Jana's chair when the waiter came over and asked if anyone wanted dessert.

"I can't eat another thing," Evie declared.

Carson chuckled. "Why am I not surprised? You should have seen the stuff she bought at the rodeo."

"Hey." Evie elbowed him. "I shared with the kids behind us."

Carson smirked, his gaze dancing with amusement.

"Do you want anything, Jana?" Knox asked close to her ear.

She rested a hand on his leg. "I'm stuffed, too."

"Want to share the lava cake? It has raspberries on it."

She glanced up at him, and he loved her knowing smile. "Okay."

"A lava cake with four forks," he told the waitress.

While she left to fulfill their order, Jana nestled closer, and Knox decided this was the best date he'd ever been on. Even though it was more of a double date, and he knew he had to talk to Jana about her dad tonight. Being here with family, plus Jana, was something he hadn't been able to expect or dream of for years.

Funny how life worked sometimes. He'd never take his relationships for granted again.

"So, Knox said you're running the jam company for your parents now that they're retired," his sister said to Jana.

Jana straightened a little. "Basically. My dad still does all the accounting, and my mom keeps the website updated. But I'm doing all the production."

Evie's brow wrinkled. "Just you? What about Natalie?"

"Oh, she's the resident family lawyer," Jana said, a tinge of hesitation in her voice. "She gives my dad legal advice, but she's not really the type to tie on an apron."

Knox loved this very thing about Jana. He trailed his fingers over her shoulder.

"Where do you sell your jam?" Carson asked.

"My dad has connections with a bunch of mom-and-pop stores in the area," she said. "He's had a couple of buyout offers, but says he wants to wait. Probably until the price is right." She picked up her drink and sipped more water.

"So your parents are here, in San Antonio, right?" Evie asked.

"Yep," Jana said.

"We should have invited them to the rodeo," Evie continued. "Knox, why didn't you offer them tickets?"

"Uh, I told him not to bother since it was such short notice," Jana cut in before he could answer. "Besides, I didn't want all the questions."

Evie's brows lifted, and she looked from Jana to Knox. "Ah. I get it. You're dating, but don't really want it to be the number one news item in Prosper."

"Right," Knox said, taking Jana's side. He'd brought up the same thing, about inviting her parents, but Jana had seemed extremely reluctant, so he'd dropped it without questioning her. "You know small towns. Especially since I don't live there, I don't want Jana hounded with questions. Or anyone else in our family."

"Makes sense," Evie said.

A short silence fell amongst the group, and Knox was pretty sure everyone was thinking of the questions that might be asked of Macie, Holt, and even Ruby.

Still . . . they all knew, and Holt had practically given Knox his blessing. Not that Knox needed it from anyone. But it had been nice, of course.

When the lava cake came, everyone dug in, even Evie.

"When are you heading back?" Evie asked Jana. "We can meet for breakfast in the morning, although it will have to be early. I have to be in the office by eight."

"I'll plan my next trip out here for longer," Jana said. "I've got to fill orders tomorrow, so I'm leaving around six."

"Okay, no problem," Evie said, then stifled a yawn. "We'd better head out."

Knox stood and hugged his sister goodbye, then shook Carson's hand. When he turned, Jana had stood as well.

"I think I'd better get to the hotel," she said. "Early morning."

Knox knew this night wouldn't last forever, but reality was hitting fast. "Okay, I'll take you to your car back at the arena. Are you sure you don't want to stay in a room at my hotel?"

She smiled. "I'm sure."

"Okay . . ." Knox paid the bill, then walked out of the restaurant with her, hand in hand. On the drive back to arena, he knew now was the time. He'd promised Holt, and timing might be important here. "Hey, I need to ask you something, and I want you to know that it's just a business question."

Jana looked at him in surprise.

He explained how Holt had secured grant money to fund the horse rehabilitations, and now that grant would be divided.

Jana said nothing as she listened, until he got to the email part that listed the company who'd claimed to have a volunteer vet. "There's only one vet in Prosper, unless they're bringing in another one, but who would do that much volunteering? Maybe a retired vet?" she said.

"Maybe," Knox said as he pulled into the arena parking lot and headed to where she'd parked. "But Holt and I looked into the equestrian company more and found that one of Prosper's local citizens is on the board of directors."

Jana's brows shot up. "Oh, wow. So they're going in

through a back door? Piggybacking on the grant work that Holt already did?"

Knox parked next to Jana's SUV. "That's Holt's theory, and maybe mine, too. But I wanted to talk to you about it first."

Jana's brow creased. "I'm not an expert in business organizations."

He released a breath, then turned to face her more fully. "Your dad is, though, and I found his name listed on the board of directors for RD & Associates."

"Really?" Jana said, her eyes widening.

Knox nodded to confirm.

Jana blinked. "Wow. I had no idea. I mean, I don't really track my dad's business." She pulled out her phone and looked up the name of the company he'd told her.

He couldn't explain the relief he felt that Jana had no knowledge of RD & Associates applying for the grant. He'd known it in his heart, but to have it verbally confirmed was even better. Jana had the board of directors' page pulled up, and she read through the list of names.

"I still don't get why they're doing this—on top of the one that's already established at Prosperity Ranch," Jana said. "You'd think they'd just apply for a grant in another location so they didn't have to split it."

"I don't understand it, either," Knox said. "But I need to help Holt find out, so when we saw your dad's name . . ." He didn't finish, because he didn't have to.

"I'm calling him right now," Jana said, pulling up her contacts.

"It's late—" Knox started, but she was already on the phone.

When her dad didn't answer, Jana sighed. "He must have his phone off."

"And he's probably asleep."

They both looked at the dash clock. It was nearly midnight.

"I'll call tomorrow morning," Jana said, "and let you know what he says. I can tell you, he's going to hear a piece of my mind." She popped open the passenger-side door and slid out before Knox could reply.

"Hey, wait up." He climbed out of the truck and reached her before she could open her SUV door.

"What?" she asked, turning.

"Did you forget something?" he said in a low voice.

Tilting her head, she said, "Like what?"

"Like . . . saying goodbye to me." He leaned close, not touching her yet, just breathing in her scent of raspberries.

Jana lifted her chin, her pretty mouth curving upward. "Goodbye, Knox."

He didn't move, didn't step back, but pointed to his cheek, indicating he was hoping for a kiss. But Jana one-upped that. She slid her arms about his neck, pressed against him, then kissed him on the mouth.

He hauled her closer and backed her against the SUV. She smiled against his mouth, and tugged his collar toward her. He used one hand to brace himself against the SUV while he continued to explore her mouth. He was pretty sure if there was something flammable nearby, it would have ignited. Kissing Jana was like holding heaven in his arms. But he was still holding back. This was a relationship he wanted to do right.

When their kissing slowed, Knox was even more reluctant to leave her.

She ran her hands over his shoulders and down his chest, putting some distance between them. "Is that a better goodbye?" she teased.

"Much better," he whispered. Burying his face against the softness of her neck, he shut his eyes, holding her close, and wondering what in the world Jana Harris had done to his heart.

And eventually, he released her and climbed back into his truck. Only when she left the parking lot did he finally head back to his hotel.

The hotel room he'd checked into was too quiet, too lonely. Knox couldn't remember a time when he'd felt this way—like he was missing a part of himself, an appendage or something. He didn't like that there were so many unknowns between him and Jana. Something had shifted tonight, though. She'd instigated more affection, and she'd been comfortable with Evie. Those were two signs of progress.

Once he settled into bed, he sent Holt a quick text updating him on the conversation with Jana and how she was going to call her dad. Holt wouldn't see the text until morning, but Knox knew his brother would read it early.

Knox shut his eyes, his mind going over the events of the night, and heck, the entire past week with Jana. He wasn't sure if he was lucky, or what, but this chance to start over with Jana flooded him with gratitude. Knox almost wished that he did have a job like his brother, the kind that kept him in one place, the kind that made it easier to build a strong relationship with a woman.

The ringing of his phone woke him up way too early. But when he cracked his eyes open, the sun had already risen, and it turned out that it was later than he'd wanted to wake up. He snatched his cell to see it was Jana.

"Hi, sweetheart," Knox rasped.

He heard a shuffling sound, then, "Knox? I'm so sorry."

The trembling in her voice told him she was crying, or had been crying. He was fully alert now. "What's wrong?

Where are you?" He pushed off the blanket and sat on the edge of the bed.

"I'm still in San Antonio," she said. "I just got done talking to my dad at his place."

Knox stilled, not liking the emotion in her tone. Did that mean they'd argued? "What did he say?"

Jana sniffled. "It's complicated, but basically, he's recommended Prosper because . . ." Her voice hitched. "I shouldn't even tell you this . . ."

"Jana," Knox said in a soft tone. "Tell me, please. I need to know everything, even if it's not pretty."

She exhaled. "I guess our fathers had words a while back. When we were dating. And my dad apparently threatened your dad. And your dad, who was mayor back then, too, didn't take to it kindly. He wouldn't approve a second general store in Prosper, one that my dad wanted to open. I had no idea about any of this until this morning." Her voice broke, and Knox hated that he wasn't with her in person.

"Wow," Knox said. "I had no idea, either." His mind was reeling, and he rose and walked to the window in the hotel room and opened the drapes. Sunlight streamed in.

"I'm sorry, Knox," she whispered.

"Hey, none of this is your fault," he said. "I'm just trying to figure all of this out and get to the root of it. Maybe bridges can be mended. What did your dad threaten my dad about?"

Jana sniffled again. "You. I mean, my dad told your dad to keep you away from me."

The breath left Knox's chest. "Because . . ." He was pretty sure he knew the reason, but he needed to hear it confirmed. He needed to know exactly what he was dealing with here.

"Your reputation," Jana said. "You know how parents can be. Things are so extreme for them."

Knox rubbed a hand over his face. His past continued to

rear its ugly head. And the stuff that happened in high school was just teenage drama, but still . . ." "I wish my dad would have told me. I don't know why he didn't." Did his mom know? Did Holt?

"It's in the past, Knox," Jana said. "And it should be water under the bridge, but apparently, my dad still has strong feelings."

"I'll say . . ."

"There's more."

Knox closed his eyes, his heart hammering.

"I told him we're dating."

He exhaled. "Good."

She was crying again.

"Jana?"

When she didn't answer, he said, "Where are you? I can come to wherever you are. I hate that you're feeling like this. You know your dad's actions are *his*, not yours."

She seemed more calm when she spoke. "I told him to cancel the grant request. He has the power to do it, but he told me he would on one condition."

Knox knew it was coming before she continued. "Please tell me you didn't."

"I did," Jana whispered. "I told him I'd break things off with you if he'd break things off on his end."

He squeezed his eyes shut. "I don't care about the grant, Jana. You're more important. Holt and I will find another solution."

"Don't you see, Knox?" Jana said. "I can't be the cause of your family's livelihood being compromised. I already promised my dad, so I think it's best for everyone and everything to call us quits. It was probably too good to be true, anyway. We can't go back and pretend nothing happened."

"I'm not trying to pretend nothing happened during

those years we didn't speak," Knox said, his shock and disbelief turning to anger and desperation. "And things aren't too good to be true. They're *real*, Jana." He took a steadying breath. "At least on my end. I'm not dating you for a fling. I'm all in, sweetheart, and I'll do whatever it takes to prove that to you."

"I don't need proof," Jana said. "I know you believe we can make it through all of this, but our fathers apparently hate each other. I just found all of this out, and I'm reeling over it, but I can see one thing clearly."

Knox wanted to break something. Punch a hole through the hotel wall. Anything that would stop the pain of his heart tearing in half.

"Knox, I'm really sorry," she said softly. "I do care for you, and maybe there was a tiny chance things would work out between us, and we'd survive the weight of our pasts, but—"

"You mean the weight of *my* past," Knox said. "Your dad wanted me to stay away from you back then, and he still wants that now. Why is *he* the one who gets his way? What about *you*, what about *me*? It's *our* lives now, not his."

"We're talking about your family's livelihood, Knox," she said in a near whisper. "I can't have this on my conscience. If I don't agree to my dad's demands, then what do you think our future will be? Full of fighting and guilt. That's no way to have a relationship. You should know."

She'd just described his marriage to Macie, and they both knew it.

Knox's throat hurt, and his eyes burned. "Jana . . . I love you. Does that count for anything?"

A heartbeat passed, then two.

"I love you, too, Knox," she whispered. "But this has to be goodbye."

15

JANA KEPT DRIVING past the road that would take her back to Prosper, and instead turned toward her sister's place. Natalie might have already left for work, but Jana had texted her that she needed an urgent meeting. So whether that was at Natalie's condo or her office, it didn't matter to Jana.

Yes, Jana might have called things off with Knox, and it still hadn't fully hit her. None of this had. And she was sure once she processed it, she'd be curled into a ball. But right now, she was furious. Things had happened years ago that she had no knowledge of, and now, it had destroyed what she and Knox had so recently and fragilely began to build together.

Was there still a future for her and Knox? Jana sincerely doubted it. There had just been too much turmoil between them. Too many misunderstandings. Too many silent years. And Jana was fully entrenched in her family's business, and she couldn't support herself on her column. So what choice did she have but to be loyal to her parents?

And Knox had to be loyal to his family, even though he was willing to overlook all of that. Jana wouldn't let him break apart his family once again. The aftermath of the first time was still haunting every step in their relationship.

A return text from Natalie buzzed Jana's phone. She read it at the next stoplight. Good. Natalie was heading back to her condo to meet. Maybe she'd already talked to their parents and knew what was coming.

Jana just hoped that her sister wouldn't put on her lawyer poker face and would instead be the sister she should be.

It took only a minute to find a parking place, since most of the residents were likely at work. Jana had been to Natalie's condo a handful of times, which spoke volumes as to their sibling relationship. All business.

Jana turned off the car, and another text chimed in. Her heart thumped when she saw it was from Knox. She closed her eyes and exhaled. She didn't even want to read it, because then she'd start bawling, and she really needed to be levelheaded. Still . . . she opened the text.

Talked to Holt and my dad. Please call me when you can.

"I can't," Jana whispered to herself. She'd barely made it through that first phone call with him, and even if somehow things could be smoothed out with the Prosper family, she'd seen the deep-seated hatred her dad had for them. It wasn't a good foundation to build any relationship upon.

Because with Knox, she knew things were real, too. Like, *marriage* real. And how would that be? Having fighting in-laws when she was raising their grandkids?

Jana should at least hear Knox out, right?

She stared at his text, her thoughts warring against each other. In the end, she decided not to reply yet. If she did, he'd just text again with something else, and she had to focus on her meeting with Natalie.

Climbing out of the SUV, Jana hurried to the condo. She found the spare key that her sister had told her about, and she let herself in. Natalie's place was so immaculate that it was almost sterile. She didn't have any plants or flowers, or anything of that sort. Black and white photographs of bridges decorated the living room wall, paired with a black leather couch and otherwise white furniture.

Jana was too antsy to sit down, though, and had paced the room a dozen times before Natalie showed up.

"Hi," Natalie said, coming into the living room, her light green eyes wary. Her strawberry blonde hair was pulled back in a smooth ponytail, and she was dressed in a power suit—navy with a white blouse beneath.

Jana always felt dowdy next to her sister, and that made her angry, too. Why did she allow herself to feel less than others in her family? Now that she'd found out the deceit and greed going on, she was even more mad at herself for never questioning anything.

"Want something to drink?" Natalie asked, heading to the kitchen. "We can sit and talk in here." No hug, nothing friendly.

Not that Jana was in the mood . . . "I'm fine." She was probably hungry, but her body wasn't focused on any of that.

A few moments later, the two sisters were sitting across from each other in an equally sterile kitchen. There was literally nothing on the kitchen counters, save for a complicated looking cappuccino maker.

"So . . ." Natalie said with a brief smile. "What's up?"

"Did you talk to Dad yet?"

The flicker in Natalie's eyes answered the question. "Look, Jana—"

"Answer me this question," Jana cut in. "Why did Dad threaten Rex Prosper? I know it was about Knox, but I want to know when, how, and why exactly. And why did *you* know and not me? He was my boyfriend, so I don't know why I'm the last to know."

Natalie looked away, her neck staining red.

Jana waited, and she'd wait as long as necessary to get the answers she wanted.

When Natalie met her gaze again, Jana was surprised to see tears in her sister's eyes.

"I found a pregnancy test in the garbage, and I told Dad," Natalie said. "I knew it had to be yours."

Heat rushed into Jana's chest, then pooled into her belly. She stood from the table, unable to sit any longer. "Why didn't you come to me?" She might be asking her sister that question, but she was berating herself for throwing it away where her sister could find it . . . which brought up other questions of how Natalie really found it.

Jana strode to the kitchen window, shaking with disbelief. She couldn't even look at her sister.

"I didn't know what to do," Natalie said. "I was shocked and scared, I guess. More scared. And I know that we haven't ever really been the best of friends, Jana. But I do love you, and I guess I was petrified for you. Remember Maggie—my friend in high school who had to drop out when she got pregnant?"

Jana didn't move, didn't answer.

She heard Natalie rise and shift a chair. "I should have asked you. Been a better big sister and warned you about getting too close to a boy. About having a boyfriend. How to have a healthy relationship that wouldn't result in a teen pregnancy."

Jana closed her eyes. Her parents had never talked to her about that stuff. It wasn't their fault she'd fallen so hard for Knox, but he'd been the first person she'd ever felt truly knew her and listened to her and cared about her. Sure, she knew her family loved her—because they had to. And maybe that had messed with her psyche, but that didn't mean Natalie should have done what she did.

Not Over You

Natalie moved closer. "Dad told me he'd take care of it and not to say a word to you or Mom."

"Why did you tell Dad, not Mom?" Jana asked, her voice raw. But she knew. Mom couldn't handle conflict. Family fights sent her to her room for days. Dad was the enforcer. Dad was the disciplinarian. Dad set down the rules.

"Dad would have found out anyway if I told Mom," Natalie said, her tone subdued. "I didn't know it would... go so far."

Jana turned then and eyed her sister. "What do you mean?"

"I was still awake the night Dad came home from talking to Rex Prosper." Natalie folded her arms, blinking back new tears. "Dad was banging things around in the kitchen, and I'm surprised he didn't wake the entire household. He told me that Rex Prosper was just as much of a bastard as his son, and no one in our family was ever to have anything to do with any member of the Prosper family."

Jana swallowed against the painful lump in her throat.

Natalie lowered her gaze. "He said that payback would be painful. Dad didn't know how or what yet, but it would happen."

"So it's come down to the grant thing for the rehabilitation project?"

Natalie's hesitation put Jana on alert.

"What?" Jana demanded. "What else has Dad done?"

Natalie moved back to the table and sat down with a heavy sigh. Panic shot through Jana when her sister dropped her head in her hands. "There's more."

Jana froze. She'd never seen her brilliant, smart sister look so defeated. "Tell me, Natalie."

"Dad has thwarted other things with Prosperity Ranch," Natalie said.

Jana wanted to run from the condo screaming. Instead, she held very still and listened.

"Dad put in some calls that resulted in lost training opportunities for Prosperity Ranch," Natalie said. "You know how things in the ranching world can be word of mouth. People recommending each other's services."

Yes, Jana did know.

"It didn't take much to tarnish the reputation of Prosperity Ranch to the larger equestrian world out there."

"Wow" was an understatement. "Wasn't one thing enough? Why does Dad have to continue holding this grudge? I was a dumb teenager, and so was Knox. It's not like we were the first teenagers in the world to make poor decisions."

Natalie rubbed the back of her neck. "I agree. And I see that now. Back then, it was about me proving to Dad that *I* was the good daughter, the smart sister. I got a weird trip out of it, and that was wrong of me. I've felt guilty about it for years, and that guilt has stopped me from reaching out to you. Because if you'd learned what I'd done, I thought you'd hate me forever."

Jana stared at Natalie. This all explained so much, but it was also completely dysfunctional. "I do hate you, but I also love you. I mean, I hate what you did." She sighed. "You were a teenager, too, so I don't totally blame it on you. Dad's reaction was completely out of line."

Natalie nodded. "That's what I told him on the drive over here."

"You did?" Jana couldn't explain the relief that filled her. Out of this entire mess, she and her sister finally saw eye-to-eye on something.

Natalie stood again and walked around the table. Placing a tentative hand on Jana's shoulder, she said, "Jana, I'm so sorry for what I did years ago. Please forgive me. And you have to know that I told Dad he needs to bury the hatchet. The past is behind us, and . . . him threatening you about Prosperity Ranch is also wrong. I also told Dad that your relationship with Knox is no one else's business. You're grown adults and can make your own decisions."

Jana saw the sincerity in her sister's eyes. "You said that to Dad?"

"I did."

Jana rose and hugged her sister. "Thank you." Then she drew away, feeling the trembling start in her limbs. "I broke up with Knox this morning."

"I'm sorry about this mess," Natalie said.

"I'm sorry, too," Jana said. More than she could probably comprehend right now.

"You should call Knox." Natalie squeezed her shoulder and offered a small smile. "Tell him it was all a misunderstanding."

"It's not that easy. There are other things that make this complicated beyond our fathers." Jana sighed. "Besides, I don't trust Dad. I'm not doing anything until I know that Dad is sticking to his word about canceling the grant request."

"Oh, he's going to stick to his word," Natalie declared.

Jana raised her brows. "How can you be sure?"

Natalie smiled. "I'm not a lawyer for nothing. I know the ins and outs of Dad's business dealings, and let's just say that I can also influence things one way or another." She stepped away and picked up her phone from the table. "Now, let's call him and let him know we've talked. No more secrecy or under-the-table deals."

Jana puffed out a breath. "Maybe we should talk to him in person. I want this all laid to rest once and for all. I don't want him blowing me off by saying he has another call coming in."

Natalie raised her brows like she was impressed. "Good idea. Let's go."

"Now?"

"Yes, now," Natalie said. "I already cleared my schedule this morning, and we can be at their place in thirty minutes."

Moments later, Jana found herself in Natalie's BMW, heading to their parents. More texts had come in. Another one from Knox: *Holt wants to talk to you, too.* He followed up with a heart emoji that Jana might have stared at for too long.

A number she didn't recognize: *This is Holt, please call me as soon as you can.*

Barb: *Hey, where are you, hon? Stopped by this morning with muffins and coffee, but your car's gone.*

Barb: *Patsy and I are going to the movies tonight. Wanna come?*

Barb: *Helloooo?*

Jana sighed.

"What's up?" Natalie asked.

Jana glanced over at her sister. This casual conversation wasn't them, and Jana wasn't used to confiding in her sister for anything. "Both Knox and Holt are texting me, wanting me to call them."

Natalie didn't say anything for a moment. "You can call if you want. Dad doesn't know we're coming, anyway."

"I don't know what to say to either of them," Jana said. "I mean, Holt is probably going to tell me that the grant doesn't matter. But it does. And I can't make promises about Dad's actions until they happen, even if you're guaranteeing it."

Natalie nodded. "All right. Call Holt back when we're done meeting with Dad. But are you sure you want to leave Knox hanging?"

"You really want me to call him right now?" Jana asked.

Not Over You

"According to Dad, he's the reason behind all of this in the first place."

Natalie reached over and rested her hand on Jana's arm. "I wish I'd come to you first. I'll regret that the rest of my life." She paused. "Call Knox back."

Jana closed her eyes. "He can wait." But her heart was telling her something different than her mind.

And as the moments passed, her heart only pounded harder. When Natalie pulled up to their parents' place, Jana said, "I'll join you in a minute."

"Okay." Natalie climbed out of the car.

Jana pressed send on Knox's contact. She didn't know what she would say, but she wanted to hear his voice.

"Hey, sweetheart," he said when he answered.

Tears sprung to her eyes at the sound of his voice. "Hi." She cleared her throat because her voice had gone tight. "I'm with Natalie, and we're walking into my parents' house in a second."

"What's going on?" Knox asked, his tone gentle.

"A lot," Jana said. "I have to go, but I didn't want you to think I dropped off the planet."

She could hear Knox's smile in his voice when he said, "Thanks for calling. Holt and I have a backup plan, so don't worry about giving in to your dad for any reason."

Jana closed her eyes. She wasn't surprised Knox would have a backup plan. Her heart soared with affection for this man who had unexpectedly returned to her life again. She didn't know what the next hour would bring, let alone the next week. "I need to go," Jana said.

"Okay," he replied, but neither of them hung up.

Finally, Jana said, "I'll call you as soon as I can, but I don't want you guys making drastic plans. It's not fair . . . And I'm going to set this right." Before Knox could reply, she hung up.

She didn't want her sister and parents having a conversation about all of this without her.

Climbing out of the car, she walked to the front door of her parents' place, her heart weighted down. Who knew that a single event in her youth could throw so much of her world off-kilter?

She didn't knock, and walked in to find Natalie standing at the front window, her arms folded. Her parents were sitting on opposite ends of the couch. It was clear her mom had been crying, and her dad looked worn out. His faded red hair was cropped short, and his normally shaved face had a few days' growth.

Her mother was immaculately put together, like usual. She was waif thin and clasped her manicured hands together.

"Jana," her mom immediately said. "How could you disrupt everything like this?"

"Hi, Mom." Jana continued into the room and took her place in the overstuffed leather chair. She leaned forward with her elbows on her knees, and focused on her dad's hazel eyes that were nearly the same color as her own. "I'm here to talk to Dad, so I'd appreciate no interruptions."

She was sure her mom would only parrot what her dad would say, anyway.

Her dad's jaw was already set, and Jana wondered what Natalie had told him so far.

"Catch me up, Natalie," she said.

Natalie nodded. "I was just telling Dad that the things he's done to undermine Prosperity Ranch could be deemed libel. In other words, he could technically be sued if Mayor Prosper was so inclined."

16

KNOX SAT ON Jana's porch steps in the early afternoon. The heat was beginning to sizzle, but a nearby tree gave him plenty of shade. He'd wait here until Jana showed up. He knew that canceling his next rodeo event was the right thing to do, but the loss of money would be painful. He was saving every penny he could, and this cancellation would set him back more. But it couldn't be helped. He was determined to speak to Jana in person.

She'd called him a few hours ago to tell him about how she and Natalie had confronted their father. A lot of stuff had come to light. Ugly stuff. Things that had gone on for years with Knox none the wiser.

Holt hadn't known about it, either.

This morning, Prosperity Ranch had been Knox's first stop in Prosper, where he sat his parents and Holt down at the kitchen table. He told them everything. From the false pregnancy test, to the rumors, to Mr. Harris finding out and threatening Rex.

Knox hated that he always seemed to be the son delivering bad news to his parents and bringing angst to the family. He'd thought his black sheep days were over, but apparently not, and now, those days were still crippling the family.

"Why didn't you tell us all this had gone on with Jana?" his mother asked.

"I was not in a great place back then," Knox said. "And being a teenager, I guess I thought I could fight through it all on my own."

His mother drew in a shaky breath. "Was this why you were so insistent on marrying Macie, even though you really didn't know each other?"

Knox couldn't look at Holt right now, and he hoped this conversation wouldn't go any farther than this table, because he didn't need another wrench in his and Macie's relationship.

"I don't know, Mom," Knox said in a quiet voice. "I would hope that without the situation with Jana, I would have stepped up to the plate with Macie. Which I did, and in the end, failed."

No one spoke for a moment. This was Knox's burden, would always be. And he'd been living with it, chipping away the weight over time, but it wouldn't ever truly be gone.

"All we can do now is move forward, son," his dad said. "We can't change the past, but with the truth out in the open, we can create a better future."

Knox rubbed at his stinging eyes and nodded.

His dad told everyone at the table about the night that Judd Harris confronted him. It was painful for Knox to hear, and painful to know that his dad had been fighting silent battles for him for so long.

Which led to a question from Knox. "Did you prevent Mrs. Harris from opening another general store in town?"

Rex had folded his hands atop the table, and said, "It's complicated."

"It's a yes or no answer. You just said we need the truth out in the open."

His dad rubbed the back of his neck.

"Rex," Knox's mom said. "We need the full truth here, or we won't know what we're dealing with."

"Mom's right," Holt said with a sigh. "We're all adults here, Dad. Spill it."

"I voted it down," Rex said in a reluctant tone, "but to be fair, so did the majority. Even if I'd changed my vote, the request would have been denied. Prosper wants to stay a small town—you know that, son."

"I do know that," Knox said. "I also know the mayor's vote is likely to sway others on the town council to vote likewise."

Rex couldn't deny that. "From what you've told us, we're more than even. In fact, Harris is way ahead of me in the cheap shots."

Holt jumped in. "This goes way past the *cheap shots*, Dad. We're talking about our livelihood—which affects the whole family."

Rex blew out a breath. "You're right," he murmured.

"So, this is what's going to happen," Knox said. Everyone focused on him. "We're going to bury the hatchet completely. Call it even on both sides."

By the stunned look on everyone's faces, he knew he'd shocked his family. So be it.

Holt spoke first. "Are you crazy? It would take me a while to calculate the numbers, but I figure we've lost thousands because of Harris."

"Believe me, I want to fight back more than anything," Knox said. "You know me, I'm not the type of person to back away from a fight, no matter who gets hurt in the process. But I've thought about this from all angles... and I've also thought about what we really want our future as a family to look like."

So, they were still stunned.

Knox swallowed against the nerves climbing his throat. "Jana assured me that the grant application will be canceled today, so this at least gives us a reprieve from that. But we all know Prosper is a small town, and the equestrian world is even smaller."

His parents both nodded. Holt just frowned.

"What are you proposing?" his mother asked.

"We need to extend an olive branch," Knox said. "I haven't talked to Jana about this, but I want to speak to Judd Harris in person. This all started with me."

Holt rubbed his jaw. "It takes two to tango."

"Jana is probably one of the sweetest women in the world, and I . . . I am far from that. So, let's call it for what it is. I created this, and I need to fix it."

"With a conversation?" his dad said.

"That's where it's going to start," Knox said.

"What about the plans we talked about?" Holt asked.

Yes, he and Holt had come up with a few things to get the ranch into the black, hopefully for good. One of the options they discussed was creating a fishing retreat and offering access to their river property. Another was to hold kids' exclusive rodeo events and training. A final option would be to rent out the barn for weddings and other events that seemed to be trending with the younger generation.

"Those are still on the table," Knox said. "I haven't talked to Jana about them yet, but I think we should explore all of the options."

Holt's blue eyes remained on Knox. "You're serious about her, aren't you?"

"Yes." There was no hesitation in his answer, but he also knew that his feelings for Jana might not be able to override her reservations.

He felt his parents' gazes on him, too, and Knox released a breath. "You might as well all know that I am serious about Jana. There are quite a few complications that you've all been a witness to. But I want her to be a part of my future—if she'll have me."

His mother covered her mouth with her hand, her eyes filling with tears. "Oh, Knox," she whispered.

His dad gave a firm nod. "Despite Jana's father's antics, I'd be right proud if things worked out with you and that young lady."

Their support meant the world to him, because the path ahead was rocky.

Now, he still waited on Jana's porch for her to show up. When he heard a car approaching, he didn't lift his head immediately, since there had been more than one false alarm during his wait.

Then his heart rate notched up, and he knew it was her. He lifted his head to see her SUV stop in the driveway. He was standing by the time she got out.

Jana stepped out of the SUV. She wore leggings and an oversized button-down shirt. Her hair was down, tumbled about her shoulders, like she'd tossed and turned as much as he had last night. No makeup or jewelry.

Knox had never seen her look more beautiful.

He leaned against the porch railing, not wanting to approach her without knowing what was going on in her mind. Jana grabbed a traveling bag out of her back seat, then walked slowly toward him, her gaze scanning his face. She said nothing, and he couldn't find any words, either.

When she neared, he straightened. In her eyes he saw . . . something that took his breath away.

Jana dropped the bag and stepped into his arms. She wrapped her arms about his waist and buried her face against his chest. Knox pulled her close and pressed a kiss against her hair. Whatever happened from here on out didn't matter, he decided, as long as he had Jana in his life.

He moved a hand in slow circles on her back, and she only nestled closer. Knox didn't want to ever repeat the conversation they'd had that morning when Jana had called things off. The fact that she was now in his arms gave him hope that he'd never had before. She'd stood up to her father, and Knox was going to make everything else right.

"I can't believe you're here," Jana murmured against his chest.

"Where else would I be?"

"On the way to Austin." She lifted her head to meet his gaze. "Don't you have another rodeo tonight?"

"I do."

Her brows furrowed. "What are you doing here? You need to get there."

Knox lifted a hand and ran his thumb along her jaw. "I'm where I want to be. With you. We have things to talk about."

Jana bit her lip. "I don't know if I have any answers about us, if that's what you're referring to."

He nodded, then moved his hand behind her neck and into her hair. "I don't want answers. I just want a chance, sweetheart."

Jana's hazel eyes welled with tears.

"Don't cry," he whispered, because his own throat was tight. "I have a lot of plans, and one of them will stick."

"Knox..."

"I'm serious," he said. "Can you hear me out?"

She exhaled and ran her hands up his chest. Touching was good. Touching was promising and meant she wasn't about to tell him to leave. When her hands reached his shoulders, she said, "Okay."

"Okay?"

She nodded, biting that lip again. He inched closer, and when she ran her fingers into his hair, he pressed his mouth lightly against hers.

The kiss was slow, but it wasn't a goodbye, it was something new. Like a seed planted in the spring, eager to grow into something stronger and more beautiful. Knox pulled her close again. Every part of his soul felt connected to Jana, and it was a heady sensation.

Jana sighed against him, then drew away. Tilting her head, she said, "Are you sure about all of this, Knox? I mean, I'm just a small-town girl, and you've got fans all over the nation. What if you get bored?"

"All that stuff out there isn't real," he said. "The bull-riding is real, sure, but not the relationships. Those people don't know who I am inside. You do."

The smallest smile appeared. "I do."

"And I'm hoping you believe me when I say all that stuff I went through is behind me," he said. "Way behind me. I wish I'd never gone through any of it, but since it led me back to you, I'm grateful."

Jana's fingers slid along his neck, then down his chest, sending a path of goose bumps across his skin. "Come on inside," she said.

She moved to grab her bag, but Knox said, "I've got it."

Her smile went straight to his heart. "Why, thank you, Mr. Bull-Rider."

He winked. "Anytime, sweetheart."

Hand in hand, they walked into her house. They headed into the kitchen, where Jana poured two glasses of water, then sat at the table.

Knox pulled his chair out and sat across from her; even though he'd rather be closer, this distance was good for what they had to talk about. "I need your parents' address," he said. "I aim to visit your dad and see if we can't get some of this stuff put behind us."

Jana's brows shot up. "I don't think that's a good idea, Knox. I mean, he's canceling the grant request, but . . ."

When she didn't continue, he filled in, "He still has a problem with me?"

"Yeah." Jana looked down at her glass of water. "I think it will soften in time, but right now . . ." She met his gaze. "I think a little more time is needed."

Knox rubbed a hand over his jaw. "If you don't want me to discuss our current relationship, then that's fine. But I need to get the past out in the open. It's the only way to clean the festering wound."

Jana looked away. "I don't know. He was livid this morning, and I think the only way I made it through that meeting was because Natalie was there. She made him toe the line, and since she's a lawyer, she can do that. I'm . . . dependent on them for my livelihood. I hate to admit it, since I'm a grown woman, but this is my job."

"I get it, I really do, but this goes back to before you were working for their jam company," Knox said. "I need to apologize to him in person; there's no other way for me to do this."

Jana closed her eyes. When she opened them, she said, "I just don't want to make it worse, you know."

"Enough time has passed since we were in high school," Knox said. "Whether or not your dad wants to face the reality of his daughter making her own choices is his issue, not yours. You decide what your choice is, and then that's what he will have to live with."

Jana exhaled and rested her hands on the table. "You sound like my sister."

Not Over You

He raised his brows. "Is that a good thing?" Her smile was half of what he wanted it to be.

"Things are getting better between us," she said. "We've had some genuine conversations today."

"Good." He reached for her hand across the table and threaded their fingers together. "Is she okay with . . . us?"

"Yeah." Jana's smile was wider now. "She's definitely okay with us."

"And you?" Knox asked. "Are you okay with us?"

Jana's eyes clung to his. He waited, and waited some more. Then she pushed up from the chair and leaned across the table.

"I'm okay with it," she whispered, then kissed him.

The table might have separated them, but he felt the full impact of her kiss anyway.

"I think that's the best thing I've heard in my entire life," Knox whispered.

Jana smiled. "You're easy to please, Knox Prosper."

"I suppose I am." He was tired of the distance the table put between them. He straightened, then moved around the table.

Jana just watched him with a gleam in her eyes. When he stepped close, she rose and looped her arms about his neck. Pressing close, Knox almost wished he didn't have anything else to do that day, or that week, for that matter.

"Come with me, or not," Knox said. "But I want to talk to him soon."

Jana pressed her lips against his neck, then looked up at him. "I have jam to make, and you have a rodeo to get to tonight."

"I've already canceled," Knox said. "I'm here for you, and I want to clean up this mess, because I'm tired of not being with you."

"You're with me right now."

Knox smiled. "I am."

17

Jana paced the kitchen as she waited for Knox to show up. When she'd found him waiting for her yesterday at her house, she was pretty sure if she wasn't already in love with him, she'd have fallen in love with him at that moment. More likely, she'd never really stopped since high school.

He'd helped her with the batches of jam, then he said he'd be staying at his parents' ranch. Apparently, their family dynamics were going well, and everyone "approved" of her. The way he told her had made her smile, because he'd followed up with, "I don't need anyone's approval about you. I've already made up my mind. But staying here would mean I'd stare at the ceiling all night wishing I could be with you, sweetheart."

Now, Jana sighed, because when Knox got here, it meant they'd be driving to San Antonio together to see her dad. At first, Jana hadn't wanted him to go, then she didn't want to be a part of the meeting, but then she'd changed her mind again. After talking to her sister the night before about all the updates, Natalie said that if Jana went with Knox, it would show how much of a united front they were.

The idea had then warmed.

Jana heard the rumble of his truck before she saw it. The

sound sent both anticipation and happiness through her heart. She was having a hard time believing that she was dating Knox Prosper again. He was back in her life, and if she were to believe all the things he'd been telling her, he was here to stay.

Well, *here* was the relevant word. She wasn't going to let him give up any part of his bull-riding career. Not after all that he'd fought for and lost in order to pursue his dream. Her phone chimed with a text from Natalie.

Jana glanced down and smiled at the message.

Good luck today with Dad. If you need me to break ankles, just call.

It was remarkable what one, single honest conversation could do for her relationship with her sister. For the first time since Jana was a young kid, she felt like she had a true sister. *LOL, I'll let you know,* she wrote back.

Jana moved to the kitchen window, where she saw Knox climb out of his truck. He wore faded jeans, a plain gray T-shirt, and a black cowboy hat. Classic Knox. She should probably just meet him on the porch, but she kind of liked him walking up her walkway and knocking on her door to pick her up.

Speaking of knocking, he'd knocked, so Jana headed to the front door. "Who is it?" she called through the door.

"The best thing that ever happened to you, sweetheart."

Jana laughed and opened the door. And there he was. Smiling his cocky grin, with his beautiful green eyes. He grasped her hand and tugged her toward him. She lifted her chin, waiting for his kiss.

She wasn't disappointed, and she slipped her hands about his neck as he thoroughly kissed her. He smelled of soap and pine and Knox, and she wanted to keep him to herself the rest of the day. She might have acted too reluctant when he

Not Over You

drew away, because he said, "Good morning to you, too," with a chuckle.

"I think I missed you, or something."

"I know I missed you, or something." He kissed her again, this time slowly, with quite a bit of lingering. "Ready?"

"Yeah," she said, unable to hold back a sigh. "Can't we just live in a bubble?"

Knox twisted a lock of her hair around his fingers. "Soon."

Jana nodded. "Okay, then, are you okay if we take my SUV?"

"Because my truck is . . ."

"Well, it's . . . you know. Great and all that. But it did break down recently."

"Whatever you want." He threaded their fingers. "I think I'll be saying that a lot with you."

She laughed. "Sounds good to me." She squeezed his hand, then said, "I'm going to grab my purse, and then we'll go."

As they drove to San Antonio, Jana's mind was full of scenarios of how her dad would act around Knox. He said he'd called and left a message on her dad's phone to let him know they'd be coming. Her dad had never responded to Knox, but Natalie had told her that their parents didn't have any traveling plans.

"You know the plans for the ranch I talked about last night?" Knox asked.

He had told her about the options that Holt had come up with, such as doing fishing retreats, kids' rodeo events, or renting out the barn for events . . . They were all great ideas, but would take a lot of work. And now that her dad had agreed to cancel the grant application, Jana hoped that the Prosper family wouldn't have to take on more work than they were already doing.

"Yeah, I remember," Jana said. "And remember how I said that I don't want my dad's actions to put more stress on your family?"

"I remember," Knox said. "But this morning, I talked more with my brother, and we both know that my bull-riding career has a time limit. So we're researching all of the scenarios, and whatever looks to make the most sense, it will be the thing I head up."

Jana glanced over at Knox to find his steady green gaze on her. "So you're going to move back to your parents' ranch?"

"Not exactly," he said. "I'd get my own place, and then be the manager over whatever project we agree on. I could work it around the bull-riding, or start full-time when I'm done with the rodeo."

Jana soaked all of this in. "You shouldn't quit the rodeo, not when it's been your dream for so long."

"I'm not quitting anytime soon," he said in a quiet voice. "But sometimes, dreams change." He lifted a hand to her shoulder, his fingers lightly stroking her neck. "Whatever happens, though, I want you to be a part of it."

The warmth from Knox's touch traveled all the way to her heart. She didn't know how to answer, she really didn't. He was saying things she didn't know if she was ready to hear. Or feel. "I don't even know what to say to that."

"I'm not asking for answers from you, Jana," Knox continued. "I'm just telling you how I feel. Plain and simple."

Jana exhaled. She wanted to pull over to the side of the road and hug this man, bury her face in his neck, feel his heartbeat against hers. For years, she'd missed Knox, but she'd completely given up on him. Yet, here he was . . .

Needless to say, Jana felt a lot of trepidation as she pulled up to her parents' home. Seeing her parents yesterday had been stressful enough, and digging up the past hadn't been fun, either.

When she parked, Knox took her hand and squeezed. "You don't have to come in."

She met his gaze, and her heart practically melted. No matter what her dad thought of Knox, or the mistakes he'd made, or any of them had made, she wanted this man in her life. Hopefully, permanently. "I'm coming."

"Okay." He leaned over and kissed her cheek. "Let's go."

So Jana walked hand in hand with Knox to her parents' place. Her mom answered the door.

Her mom's eyes looked as wide as an owl's as her gaze landed on Knox. Jana guessed that her dad hadn't informed her mom of the phone call. And now, she wondered if her dad had gotten the message.

"Hi, Mom," Jana said. "You remember Knox Prosper?"

Her mom's gaze moved to Jana's hand in Knox's. "Of course, I remember you, Knox. Uh, come in, you two. I'll get Dad."

She hurried off, leaving Jana to open the door and walk in with Knox. Of course, her mother wouldn't want to have a conversation alone with them. But Jana didn't mind; it was her dad they needed to confront.

"Your mom seems . . ."

"Frazzled?" Jana suggested.

"That's a good word for it," he said. "Not that I spent much time around your parents, but I don't remember her being so skittish."

"She's gotten more that way over the years," Jana said. "She hates conflict and avoids it at all costs."

Knox merely nodded.

Jana led him into the living room, and Knox checked out

the pictures on the wall. There were several of Natalie, at her various graduations—high school, college, and law school. Another few from a rare family vacation. Jana's high school graduation picture was on the wall, but it was the only picture of her in the whole place, that she knew of. Jana had been the daughter her parents had tolerated more than anything.

And she supposed they were still tolerating her. They didn't even want to live in the same town anymore. But those were issues that Jana would deal with another day. This moment was about what Knox wanted to say.

She and Knox sat on the couch together not saying anything, their hands linked, Knox absently rubbing his thumb over her wrist.

They waited almost ten minutes before her father came down the stairs. She assumed his office was on the second floor. She'd never explored her parents' place. But what had taken her dad so long?

Knox released her hand and rose to his feet when her dad entered the room. Her dad was dressed in a suit and tie, which made Jana frown. Was he trying to intimidate Knox or something, or was he on his way to a business meeting? She'd rarely seen him so dressed up.

"You came, too?" her dad said, his gaze moving from Knox to her. He'd completely ignored Knox's outstretched hand.

"I can wait somewhere else if you want your conversation to be private with Knox," Jana said, already feeling her neck heat up.

"I have nothing to hide," her dad said, his gaze slicing to Knox. "Never did."

This wasn't completely true, and her dad knew it.

Her dad took a seat on the chair opposite the couch. Leaning back, he folded his hands. "What was so important that we need to have this discussion again?" Once again, he was looking at Jana.

She bit her lip and looked over at Knox. He'd taken his seat again, and she could practically see the tension vibrating in his shoulders.

"I wanted to speak to you in person, man to man," Knox said in a calm tone.

Her dad scoffed. "A man doesn't live recklessly. He takes his responsibilities seriously. And you're not that man, Mr. Prosper. I might not be able to tell you what to do, or my daughter for that matter, but that's not going to stop me from still trying."

Knox ran a hand over his face. "I know I hurt your family," he said. "I didn't know the extent until recently, and for that, I'm even more sorry."

Jana could see the surprise in her dad's eyes, even though he didn't react outwardly.

"Jana told me what you agreed to do yesterday about canceling the grant," Knox continued. "And for that, I'm grateful. I don't work at Prosperity Ranch right now, but I hope to in the future. Things between me and my family have been on shaky ground for a while, but I'm working hard to repair it."

Her dad's brows furrowed. "How does your ex-wife feel about you being back at the ranch?"

Knox didn't answer for a moment, and the tension in the room seemed to heat up. "I haven't discussed that with Macie directly, but I've spoken to my brother—"

"You mean your ex-wife's husband," her dad cut in. "Ha, what a mess."

"Dad," Jana cut in next.

He shot her a glare, and she glared right back.

"As I was saying," Knox said, "Holt and I haven't always

seen eye to eye on things, and that will probably never change, but we both agree that family comes first. That's our end goal. So what happens at Prosperity Ranch is very much my business, and when I retire from rodeo, I'll figure out a way to contribute and grow the ranch's profitability."

Her dad leaned forward. "You telling me you're quitting rodeo?"

"Not yet, but it's not a lifelong career, as you know."

Lines creased her dad's forehead. "What about your other responsibilities?"

"Which?"

"Your kid," her dad said, the hardness back in his tone. "Seems like you think nothing of knocking up girls, then dumping them. It's a despicable pattern—no better than a dog's life."

Jana covered her mouth.

"What happened with Jana and I was a mistake," Knox said. "Not because we were together, but because we let others do the talking for us. I believed false information and let that make my decisions for me. I want you to know, sir, that *Jana* was never a mistake. If she'd become pregnant, then I wouldn't have turned my back on her, or any kid of ours."

Her dad's jaw worked, and Jana's stomach felt like it was about to turn inside out.

"You might be sorry now, Prosper," her dad said. "But that doesn't make life all roses and daisies. You're still a lowlife."

Jana's eyes stung with tears, and she had no idea how Knox could sit there and take her dad's harsh words.

Knox had gone very still, and when he next spoke, it was devoid of any emotion. "You have every right to your own opinion, and I hope to prove you wrong someday."

"I'm not just talking about my daughter," her dad said.

Not Over You

"You married that Macie woman and then skipped out on her, too. In my opinion, Prosperity Ranch would be better off without the likes of you. Moral character goes a long, long way in my book."

"I'm glad to hear that," Knox said, a bite in his tone. "And I'm glad it took Natalie to call you out on your own cut corners, so we can all keep our moral characters in line."

Jana had never seen her dad's face so red.

"You stay out of my business!" he said in a seething tone. "Stay out of my family, and anything with the Harris name on it!"

Knox stood, and Jana felt sick. He was going to leave. She knew it. Walk out of this house, and right out of her life.

Her dad rose to his feet, too, and if this wasn't so upsetting, it might be comical. Her dad had put on the pounds over the years, and Knox looked like he was strong enough to wrestle a bear to the ground—or a bull.

"I love your daughter, sir," Knox said. "I always have. Life took a hard detour for me, and those are regrets I will always have to live with. But if she chooses to be in a relationship with me, then I can promise you and your wife that Jana will *always* be my priority. She will always come first, no matter what. And I'll treat her like the amazing and talented woman she is."

Tears fell down Jana's cheeks, and she couldn't take a full breath.

Without waiting for her dad's reply, Knox turned to her and held out a hand. "Ready, sweetheart?"

Jana felt a rush of emotion swell in her chest. She wiped at her tears, then placed her hand in his. Knox smiled and drew her to her feet.

She faced her dad, and said, "Dad, you're wrong about Knox. Dead wrong. And I hope that you'll forgive me and

Knox someday. Anger and bitterness are no way to live your life, and I'm speaking from experience."

Her dad looked down at the ground, not meeting her gaze.

Together, Jana and Knox walked out of the door, hand in hand. Jana hoped her dad would find a way to look beyond past mistakes and stop using them to hurt others. But for now, she had to give him space. If he came around, good. If not, she'd have a new family.

18

KNOX LOOKED OVER to where Jana sat in the stands among several hundred other people. He picked her out quickly, because she'd told him she'd be wearing a red cowboy hat. The thought made him smile, because she'd called it her raspberry hat.

It had been three weeks since they'd had the confrontation with her dad. Things hadn't gotten much better as far as her family went, but they hadn't gotten worse. So Knox counted that as a win. Jana was still making her jam, and writing her book and column. Knox was showing up in Prosper every chance he got during the week, but on the weekends, he'd been locked into riding bulls. He hadn't won every night, but most nights, he came away with a win, and his track record was getting a lot of attention in the pro-rodeo world.

The winnings purse just kept growing. He'd paid off Holt in full, and even put down money to invest in the current operations of the ranch.

Knox focused on Jana in the arena crowd. He couldn't help the grin that grew on his face when she waved at him. He nodded, then hearing his name announced, he climbed into the bull pen. The crowd was energetic tonight, and cheers and screams echoed around him, but he was already focused up on the beast of a bull he was about to ride.

Code Red was the bull's name, and he'd only been ridden eight seconds twice before. He was probably in the top five in the circuit, and Knox had yet to ride him. He was positive this bull would be awarded bull of the year with its 94% buck-off rate.

"Knox Prosper riding for the big win tonight and the big money," the announcer boomed into the microphone. "We're expecting a long ride with this top bull-rider. Code Red always goes to the right with a lot of buck, and really high kicks."

Knox braced himself on the top of the gate with his left arm, and he slid his right hand under the leather strap. Then he grabbed the rope handed to him, leveled it against his palm, and then wrapped it around again. Gripping the double rope, he slipped it between his last two fingers for added grip. The gate opened, and Code Red flew out of the pen.

Code Red was fast and furious as Knox moved with the bull beneath him, focusing all his attention on staying fluid and upright. The seconds sped by, and Knox barely registered any of the crowd or what the announcer said. It was just him and the beast. The bull would ultimately win, but Knox just had to hang on for eight of those seconds. When the eight-second buzzer rang, Knox released his grip to land on his knees in the dirt, only feet away from the bucking legs.

The crowd was screaming, and Knox scrambled to his feet away from the still-furious bull.

"Knox Prosper has just shown the world a perfect ride!" the announcer said. "Code Red had what seemed to be an insurmountable resume. Twenty-one straight buck-offs. But Knox Prosper rode like he had nothing to lose."

Knox moved to the arena railing, tugging off his helmet

and waving it to the cheering crowd. The crowd was deafening, and Knox walked the arena, pumping his fist into the air. But he was looking at one particular woman who was waving her red cowboy hat.

"We saved the best for last, folks," the announcer said. "And with a score of 93.6, Knox Prosper will take home the championship tonight."

More cheering and screams, and Knox acknowledged the fans, figuring he made a few new ones tonight. Elation soared through him, but he was impatient for the final announcements to finish so he could find Jana. He'd just won enough to put a down payment on a house. He paused as the other bull-riders congratulated him, but he continued moving forward.

"Knox!" someone yelled.

He only waved. Others called his name, but he was focused on the woman who'd just reached the bottom of the stands. Jana had her red cowboy hat back on and looked as pretty as a picture. Her smile was stunning, and her eyes sparkled.

In a few strides, he'd reached her. He snaked his hands around her waist, and her hands went to each side of his face.

"You were amazing!" she said with a laugh. "I can't believe you didn't fall off."

"When have you ever seen me fall off?" he teased. "Okay, don't answer that." Tugging her close, he lifted her against him, then kissed her. Nice and easy.

"They said you won the top purse," Jana said, a blush on her face. "Is that true?"

"Sure is, sweetheart."

"So are you going to get a new truck now?"

Knox chuckled. "You sound like my brothers." He leaned his forehead against hers, ignoring the people surrounding them, calling for his attention. "I'm doing something much better."

Someone clapped a hand on his shoulder, and he turned to see one of his rodeo buddies, Scott White.

"Nice job, man," Scott said. "You took that bull to task."

"It was a decent ride," Knox said with a smile. "Might have been a bit of luck involved, too."

Scott chuckled, then his attention shifted to Jana. "This your lady, Prosper?"

"Yessir." Knox reached for her hand, linking their fingers. "This is Jana Harris. Jana, this is Scott White." He was surprised to see her eyes widen.

"Oh wow," she said. "You're a legend. It's *so* great to meet you."

Scott grinned. "Why thank you, ma'am. The pleasure is all mine." He tipped his hat, and Knox supposed the guy was good-looking and had a way with the ladies.

Jana's smile ramped up a notch, and Knox frowned.

"We'll catch up later, Scott," he said in a pointed tone.

Scott laughed. "All right, I hear you, man. Congrats again."

Knox waved him off, then turned to Jana. "I thought you didn't follow rodeo."

Jana's smile went coy. "I don't, but that was Scott White. Everyone knows him."

Knox searched her gaze, knowing it was ridiculous to let this get under his skin. But Jana was a beautiful woman, and Scott had definitely noticed.

Jana lifted up on her toes, and with her mouth close to his ear, she said, "You have nothing to be jealous of, Mr. Bull-Rider."

He moved his hand up her back. "I didn't think so, but it's good to hear all the same."

Not Over You

A decent line had formed of fans waiting to greet him. Jana noticed and grinned. "I'll just wait somewhere while you greet all these fans."

"Stay with me." He grasped her hand.

So he greeted fans and signed autographs with her at his side, which was just how he wanted it. When they were down to the last few people, he looked up to see his brother Lane and sister Cara. He had no idea they were coming. This was the first rodeo outside of Prosper they'd come to.

Cara looked the most like his mom, blonde and statuesque. And Lane was blond and blue-eyed, too. They both stepped forward and hugged him.

"You guys remember Jana Harris?" Knox asked.

Lane and Cara both looked at each other, then Cara said, "Great to see you, Jana." She stepped forward to hug Jana, who Knox was sure was just as surprised as he was.

"Great to see you again, Jana," Lane said, extending his hand to shake hers. "We thought you might be here, too, but we weren't sure." By the gleam in Lane's eyes, Knox was pretty sure he'd known.

Apparently, someone else in the family had told his siblings about Knox dating Jana.

Knox slipped his arm around Jana's waist, letting her know that they were in this together.

"Don't you live in Dallas, Cara?" Jana asked.

"Sure do," she said. "Lane and I coordinated schedules so we could come to this rodeo, though. Got the night off from culinary school."

Knox had told Jana about his sister being in some fancy culinary school, and Lane would be graduating in finance soon. He'd been the one to originally secure the grant for Prosperity Ranch.

"Well, it's great to see you both," Knox said. "Do you want to join us for dinner?"

"I have a late flight, and Lane's taking me to the airport," Cara said.

Knox frowned. "Are you sure? I can get everyone hotel rooms if you want to stay overnight."

Cara only smiled. "It's all right. I've already got the flight booked, but thank you. And you two have a good night."

Lane said something similar. He'd be driving back to college, where he was doing a summer internship in the finance department.

It seemed as soon as Cara and Lane had shown up, they were gone.

"Did they not tell you they were coming?" Jana asked, looking up at him.

Finally, the arena was almost empty, and the fans dispersed.

"I had no idea," Knox said. "I wonder why they didn't tell me, or why they aren't staying longer."

Jana shrugged. "Maybe they just wanted to see if the rumors about us are true."

Knox smiled down at her. "And what rumors would that be?"

"That we're dating?"

He raised his brows. "Is that all? I thought maybe it would be something more. You know, something to warrant my two siblings making plans to come check you out."

"Me?"

"Yep."

Jana puffed out a breath, but her eyes were dancing with amusement. "Why me? Why not you?"

He drew her a little closer and bent to brush his lips against her neck. When he lifted his head, he said, "They already know me, and believe me, I'm not their favorite brother. But you . . . well, you're the main attraction in my family right now."

"I guess I can live with that, if you're okay with it."

He kissed the edge of her jaw. "I'm okay with it."

Her arms snaked around his neck, and he loved the affection she showed toward him. More and more, he knew she was comfortable with them as a couple. And he was hoping this night might work in his favor, because he had something pretty important to run by her. He'd had a phone call with her dad earlier that day, one that Jana needed to hear about. Frankly, Knox was surprised the man answered the phone, but it made it all the easier to make a business proposal.

"So, if you're hungry, we can go eat," he said. "Or just hang out."

"Let's go eat," she said. "Because I'm pretty sure you're starving."

He laughed. "You're right. And I'm glad you came."

Her hazel eyes studied him. "Me, too."

It wasn't until after they'd found a small restaurant where they secluded themselves into a booth that Knox decided to take the plunge. The restaurant was quiet because of the late hour, and their waitress seemed to be more intent on flirting with a fellow employee than keeping their drinks filled.

"So, I have a confession to make," Knox said, reaching for Jana's hand.

Her forehead furrowed. "Should I be worried?"

"I hope not." He ran his thumb over her wrist. "I talked to your dad today."

Immediately, she stiffened. "You did?"

"Yeah. I can't believe he answered my call, but he was a lot more calm than the last time I, uh, talked to him."

Jana still looked confused. "Why did you call him?"

"Well, here's the thing," Knox began, "and maybe I should have ran this past you first, but I wanted to know if my offer was even a possibility."

Her hazel eyes were solely focused on him.

"I asked him if he might be willing to sell his house."

Jana's lips parted as she stared at him.

"To me," he said. "Or I should say, to *us.*"

"Knox . . . why would you make an offer on my parents' house?"

"You know how I feel about you, sweetheart."

Her eyes filled with tears, and he wasn't sure if that was a good thing or a bad thing. She bit her lip, and tears spilled onto her cheeks.

"I love you, Jana," he said. "More each day, as impossible as it might sound. But it's the truth. I want you to be my wife, and I want us to live in Prosper. Raise our kids there. So I thought . . . maybe . . . that we could just buy your parents' house."

Jana wiped at her tears, and Knox's heart thundered with every second that passed without her response.

"You don't have to answer me yet if you don't want to," he finally said. "I know it's a lot to take in. But I know my heart, and my mind, and it's not going to change. I can wait as long as you need—"

Jana tugged him close and wrapped her arms about his neck. Pressing her face against his skin, she murmured, "I love you. And I think buying my parents' house would be perfect, too."

Relief cascaded over him like a warm waterfall as he closed his eyes and held her close. "Are you sure, sweetheart? Absolutely sure?"

"Yes, I'm sure," she whispered.

Knox was grinning, and he felt like laughing. Jana was everything to him, and now his future was filling with light. "So if I get you a ring, you're going to be happy, right?"

She drew away enough to meet his eyes. Cradling his face with both hands, she said, "A ring from you would make me the most happy woman on earth."

Knox kissed her then. After all, they were practically the only ones in the restaurant.

When he finally dropped her off at her hotel room, Knox headed back to his own room, knowing there was one phone call he couldn't delay. It was pretty late, but if she didn't answer, he'd leave a message for her to call him in the morning.

Sitting on the edge of the hotel room bed, he called his ex-wife.

When Macie answered, he almost regretted calling. This was a lot harder than he expected, and his breathing was already erratic.

"Is everything okay?" she asked immediately.

"Yeah, I'm fine." Memories surfaced of him calling her late in the past—usually telling her that his truck had broken down, or that he'd been injured in a rodeo, or busted up in a bar fight. "I just needed to tell you something before it gets back to any other members of the family."

"Okay..."

He heard the hesitation and curiosity in her voice. Another deep breath, and he said, "I'm going to ask Jana Harris to marry me." Well, he practically had, but he was going to do this right this time.

Macie didn't say anything for a long moment. Knox closed his eyes, able to imagine all of the thoughts and emotions that must be going through her mind, since she knew Jana was his high school girlfriend.

"Holt told me that you two were dating again."

He didn't miss the "again" reference. "Yeah. We reconnected when I was there a few weeks ago for the Prosper Rodeo."

"That sounds . . . fast."

What had been fast was Knox and Macie's relationship. He and Jana had a lot more longevity if he counted high school dating. "I don't know when it will happen, but I didn't want you to be blindsided."

"I appreciate the call," Macie said, her voice calm.

Knox was grateful for that. Maybe she could even be happy for him one day. "All right then, have a good night, Macie."

"You, too." Her voice was now fainter.

Just as he was about to hang up, she said, "Knox?"

He brought the phone back to his ear. "Yeah?"

"It was always her, wasn't it?"

His stomach felt like it had dropped off a high building. How could he answer a question like this to his ex-wife? They had a child together.

"Macie . . ." he rasped.

"It's okay," she said. "You don't have to answer or explain. I get it. I truly do. Life doesn't always go as planned, but in the end, if we can circle back to happiness, then that's all we can hope for, right?"

Knox didn't know if he was relieved, or more heartbroken. "Right."

There was a long pause, then Macie clicked off.

Knox remained sitting on the edge of the bed for a long time. Wishing there didn't have to be so many lessons learned and so much pain to get there. But he would hold onto Macie's words. Circling back to happiness. That, he was going to do.

19

JANA TYPED THE last sentence of her novel—at least what she thought was the last sentence. She could hardly believe she'd finished writing another book. Closing her laptop, she leaned her head back on the pillows she'd stacked up on the couch. Then, slowly, the exhilaration took over. She was done. Truly done. Well, except for revisions. But she'd gotten this far.

She sent Knox a text, because if anyone should know, it was him. He'd asked about her book every day, and she'd even read more chapters to him.

Finished writing last chapter!

His reply came a few minutes later. *You're amazing. Read it to me tonight.*

She smiled, her heart doing a somersault. *I don't know, maybe. I might need to let it sit for a few days.*

I can be persuasive.

Jana laughed. *I'll think about it . . .*

The clock on her laptop told her she only had an hour to get ready before Knox came to pick her up. They were going to dinner . . . at his parents' house. And . . . Holt, Macie, and Ruby would be there, too.

Knox had wanted this event to happen for a couple of weeks, but Jana had always made up an excuse. Knox hadn't been fooled, but he was apparently the most patient man on the planet. So when he'd called her that morning, bright and early, which was her favorite time to talk to him—his morning voice was to die for—Jana had finally consented.

It was time to grow up.

Face their future together.

If she was going to marry Knox Prosper, which she was wholeheartedly planning on, she needed to become a part of his family. And that meant his daughter's life, too, which by extension meant having a conciliatory relationship with his ex-wife. There was no getting around her, since Macie was married to Holt. It wasn't like they'd cross paths only once in a while, and Prosper was too small of a town to keep their distance.

Jana set her laptop aside and rose from the couch. What did one wear to a dinner with one's future in-laws and boyfriend's ex? A blouse and jeans? A dress?

Her phone rang, and Jana wasn't sure if this was the worst timing in the world or the best, but Barb's number lit up the screen. Jana decided to answer, because she really did need girlfriend advice. She hadn't told Barb how far things had progressed with Knox, but she knew they were dating, which brought on enough speculation, anyway.

"Hey, you up for Racoons tonight?"

"Can't," Jana said. "Knox is coming into town." They both knew that Knox refused to enter the bar scene any longer. This was just one thing that Jana was proud of him for. He knew his limits, and he also knew not to even test himself.

"Ooo," Barb said. "Things getting serious, hon?"

"I don't know," Jana said, reluctant to spill everything. "We're, uh, going to his parents' for dinner." Might as well tell her now, because Barb would likely find out from Knox's mom, Heidi, or even Macie. The three were all friends. Which was kind of funny, since Holt Prosper was one of the many men Barb had had a crush on. Come to think of it, that number likely included Knox, too.

"Shut the front door," Barb exclaimed. "Knox Prosper is taking you to a *family* dinner?"

"That's right." Jana headed down the hallway to her bedroom.

"Jana!"

"What?" she said, a smile sneaking onto her face.

"You little vixen," Barb said. "You've been holding back, hon, and I want *all* the details."

Jana laughed. "Sorry, I'll never give you all the details."

Barb groaned. "Fair enough. But tell me as much as you can. I'm dying with curiosity here."

"Tell you what," Jana said. "Help me choose an outfit, and I'll tell you some details. But you have to swear to keep them private. Don't even tell Patsy."

"Cross my beating heart," Barb said in an eager tone.

Jana switched the phone call to Facetime and showed Barb some outfit options.

"I'm assuming Macie and Holt will be there?" Barb said through the phone.

"Yep."

"And Ruby?"

"Yep."

"Wow." Barb shook her head, making her dangling earrings swing. "Knox has it bad for you."

Jana bit her lip . . . Hearing Barb say that made it all a little surreal.

"Go with the polka dot summer dress," Barb said. "Pretty, yet casual. And Knox won't be able to keep his eyes off you."

Jana felt her neck warm. "I don't want too much

attention. His parents will be there, you know. And Macie. I mean, I know who Macie is, but we've never talked. What if there is tension? Like, that weird kind of tension?"

"Listen to me, hon," Barb said as Jana pulled the dress out of the closet and inspected it to see if it needed ironing. "You walk in there, head held high. You aren't responsible for Macie or Knox's choices in the past. Their marriage is long over, and you are Knox's woman now, so be proud of that."

Jana sighed. "Sounds like something you could pull off, not me."

"Oh, honey, Knox has never been interested in me," Barb said with a laugh. "You need to know he wouldn't be taking you to his family dinner if he wasn't serious."

Jana went quiet.

"Jana . . . ? Has he said something else about this?"

She met Barb's gaze in the phone. "He says he's serious about us."

Barb hooted. "It's about time! I saw this coming a mile away. Remember what I said that night we knew he'd arrived in town for the rodeo? And how you were so feisty, then left Racoons early?"

Barb didn't forget a thing. And Jana wasn't going to remind her friend that she'd also said that Knox was still in love with his ex-wife. Which was something Jana didn't want to ever wonder about. "Well, I don't know what any of that has to do with tonight."

"It's because somehow, you subconsciously knew that Knox was about to walk into your life again."

Jana puffed out some air. Barb and her theories and conjectures. "I don't know about that. And I also wonder if I should just wear jeans."

"No way, hon, the dress is a must."

"All right."

Barb beamed. "See, that was easy. I wish I could get an invite to the dinner, too. What I wouldn't give to be a fly on that wall tonight."

Jana laughed.

"Can you promise to call me after?" Barb asked. "I won't be able to sleep unless I hear all the dirt. Both good and bad."

"All right," Jana said. "I'll call you, or text, or something."

By the time Jana was off the phone with Barb, had ironed the summer dress, and zipped it on, she only had ten minutes left. She'd have to rush through her hair and makeup routine and hope that Knox wasn't early.

Which he usually was. Something that Jana found charming.

The familiar rumble of a truck sounded outside, and Jana hurried to the kitchen window. Knox was here. She'd have to make him wait, she decided. But she didn't leave the window just yet, because Knox had just climbed out of his truck, a bouquet of red roses in his hand.

Jana's heart wobbled.

Knox strode up the walkway, wearing a black cowboy hat, black jeans, boots. He was dressed about as formal as she'd ever seen him. Oh boy.

Her breathing felt erratic as she moved to the front door. She opened it a crack to see Knox's green eyes shift to her. His gaze perused her, and his slow smile started to grow.

"I'm not ready," she said, keeping the door a crack. "Can you give me a few minutes?"

"Sure thing, sweetheart," he said, "but you look perfect."

She drew the door open another inch. "Thank you, but I'm still not ready."

He set his palm against the door and pushed it slowly open, his gaze never leaving hers. She didn't move as he stepped closer and leaned down. His lips pressed warm against hers, and her pulse went wild. One arm slipped about her, drawing her hips against his. She should keep this greeting brief, or it would take even longer to get ready.

But Knox smelled amazing, and he'd shaved, and his mouth was slowly exploring hers, making her change her mind about all kinds of things. "Knox," she breathed. "You're gonna wrinkle my dress."

His chuckle was low, and he whispered, "Then wear jeans."

Jana pushed against his chest. "I'm not spending more time trying to decide what to wear."

Knox met her gaze, amusement in his eyes. "Is that why you're behind in getting ready?"

"No, well, yes," she said. "But you're early, too."

"Didn't want these to dry out." He lifted the bouquet he was holding in his other hand.

"They're beautiful," Jana said. "What's the occasion?"

Knox's green eyes narrowed. "You're kidding, right?"

She lifted her brows. "Dinner at your parents'?"

He chuckled. "This had nothing to do with dinner or my parents." He pressed a kiss on her forehead, lingering. "I wanted to get my woman flowers because she just finished writing a book. That's reason enough."

"Hmm." Jana took the flowers and breathed them in. "I love them."

Knox grasped her hand. "I can put them in water if you still need to get ready."

"Okay." She handed the roses back to him, then she led him inside the house. "There's a vase in the cupboard above the refrigerator," she said over her shoulder as she headed down the hall.

Jana realized she was quite nervous when she couldn't figure out how to do her hair. Finally, she pulled it back into a ponytail with some wavy hair hanging by her ears. Then she added a layer of mascara and decided that was good enough. She didn't want to be too dolled up, since she didn't want to look like she was trying too hard.

She took a couple of deep breaths before heading down the hall. She stopped as soon as she reached the kitchen. Knox hadn't put the roses into a single vase, but instead had filled a dozen mason jars with water. Each jar held a rose, and he'd put the jars all about the kitchen.

"Wow." She didn't know whether to laugh or swoon.

Knox was leaning against the counter, his arms folded, eyes on her. "Couldn't find that vase."

She frowned and turned toward the fridge, then opened the cupboard above it. The vase was in plain sight. "It's right here." She looked over her shoulder to see him smiling.

"I think I like my way better," he said with a wink.

She shut the cupboard and turned. "I do, too."

He chuckled. "We'd better get a move on, or I'm not going to be able to share you with anyone tonight."

The intensity in his green eyes was doing funny things to her stomach.

"Good idea," she said.

Knox straightened and walked toward her, slowly, then stopped right in front of her. "You look beautiful."

"You do, too," she whispered. Then she stepped away. "We're going to be late."

Knox snatched her hand, then linked their fingers. "Come on."

The drive to Prosperity Ranch was much too short, and Jana's heart rate still hadn't slowed down by the time they walked up the porch steps. But Knox's hand holding hers should help. She just had to keep her head held high like Barb had told her.

"Don't worry so much," Knox whispered. He kissed her cheek, then opened the door.

They walked into the front room of the quaint country-style house. Mayor Prosper greeted them first. He wore his usual starched button-down shirt and giant belt buckle. Jana shook his hand, but then was surprised when he pulled her into a hug.

"Welcome, Jana," he said in a gruff voice.

"Daddy!" Ruby squealed, barreling out of the kitchen. She ran full tilt into Knox's legs, and he barely kept his balance.

"Hey there, little lady. Where are you going so fast?"

"To see you!"

Knox chuckled and scooped her up into his arms.

"You look pretty," Ruby said in a frank voice, looking at Jana.

"Why, thank you, Ruby," she said, the tension in her chest easing just a bit. That was a kid's doing, she supposed. "You look very pretty, too. I love your sparkly headband."

Ruby beamed and touched her headband. "Grandma bought it for me because I was good in the store."

Jana smiled, but she saw the shift in Knox's gaze.

She looked toward the kitchen. Macie was standing there, her dark hair waved about her shoulders. She wore jeans and a white and red top, and honestly could have been a model for a home and country magazine.

Holt appeared right behind her and placed a hand on her shoulder. Jana didn't miss the natural way that Macie leaned into her husband.

"Hi, Jana, welcome to the ranch," Holt said.

"Yes, welcome," Macie said with a smile.

"Thanks, everyone," Jana said, although she was starting to feel nervous again.

Not Over You

"Well, things are ready," Heidi Prosper said, coming into the room. She was an elegant blonde woman, dressed in a pink blouse and tan slacks. Jana had heard plenty about her legendary cooking skills. "Hello there, Jana."

"Hi, Mrs. Prosper," Jana said. "Thank you for inviting me to your home."

"Call me Heidi," she said with a soft smile, her gaze flitting to Knox. "And you're welcome anytime, Jana. We're happy to have you."

Heidi ushered them all to the table. Jana was glad to be sitting next to Knox. And after grace was said, Jana fielded several questions from Heidi and Rex. Macie remained quiet for the most part, except when she interacted with Ruby.

Things weren't so bad, Jana told herself.

Knox kept his arm slung around the back of her chair and didn't seem to have a problem sticking close to her. And Jana didn't notice any shared glances between Knox and his ex. Their interactions all seemed polite, or careful, if that was a better way to describe it. But their shared adoration of Ruby was obvious.

Speaking of Ruby, she was both precocious and cute at the same time. Jana found herself laughing more than once.

"Can I tell them about your book, sweetheart?" Knox whispered close to her ear.

Surprise jolted through her. "Uh, I guess."

Knox grinned, then he said, "Jana and I have an announcement to make."

Heidi's fork clattered to her plate, and everyone went absolutely silent.

Knox chuckled. "It's not what you're thinking . . . Jana finished her book today. So I'd like to make a toast to her publishing future."

Jana was positive she'd turned fire-engine red. Everyone in the family picked up their glass and congratulated her.

"Thank you." She felt both embarrassed and proud in the same moment.

Knox clinked their glasses, then drank water from his. He leaned close and whispered, "You're amazing, did I tell you that?" Then he kissed her on the cheek, in front of his entire family. It was a completely friendly, innocent kiss, but Jana still felt like she was burning up inside.

Somehow, she made it through the rest of the meal without blushing again, and everyone congratulated her once more as she and Knox prepared to leave.

"Come over anytime," Heidi told Jana. "We know Knox's traveling schedule is intense right now, but that doesn't mean you need to be a stranger."

Jana was truly touched, but there was no way she was hanging out at Prosperity Ranch without Knox. Not that she'd tell that to Heidi.

Rex gave her another hug. Holt shook her hand. Macie waved goodbye. But Ruby stole the show by wrapping her tiny arms about Jana's legs and not wanting to let go. Everyone laughed, and Jana left the ranch feeling like maybe things would be okay at these family gatherings. She'd find her place, and not be the odd woman out.

On the drive back to her place, Jana's mind raced with all the conversations she'd had, and she wondered if she could have done things better or differently. There was no going back now, and Knox seemed content with everything.

The sun had set, but splashes of gold across the sky bathed the small ranch house in warm orange. Knox parked and climbed out, then motioned for Jana to come out on the driver's side. He helped her out of the truck, then walked her to the front door, keeping ahold of her hand. They walked up the porch steps in silence, and at the top, Knox paused and looked down at her, his green eyes unreadable. "My family loves you, and I'm not surprised."

"Well, at least Ruby does."

Knox's smile was soft as he drew her close. "Not just Ruby." He kissed the top of her head. "You know, my mom was serious about you being welcome there anytime."

Jana met his gaze. "Yeah, and that was sweet of her. But going over there randomly feels too . . . I don't know . . . family-like? It's not like we're engaged or married."

Knox's gaze seemed to intensify. "About that . . ."

Jana's breath stalled as he released her hand and knelt on one knee before her. She could only stare as he reached into his pocket and pulled out something small and round and sparkly.

"Knox," she whispered.

He smiled, but as he held up the ring, his hand trembled. "Jana Harris . . . you are the love of my life." He exhaled. "Will you marry me, sweetheart?"

Jana already knew her answer, but standing here, with Knox kneeling in front of her holding up a beautiful ring, made her wonder if she had even breath left to speak a simple word.

She leaned down and rested a hand on Knox's cheek, then kissed him. He rose to meet her kiss, pulling her close. She pressed into him, loving how his arms around her had become her true home.

"Is this an answer?" Knox whispered, drawing away to meet her gaze, "or is that still coming?"

She gave a half-laugh. "It's a *yes.*"

He grinned. "Then you better see if this fits."

"Okay." She was the one trembling now as he slid the ring

onto her left ring finger. The diamond and platinum setting were gorgeous. "When did you pick this out?"

"A couple of weeks ago."

"What? Are you serious?"

"I'm serious about *you*." Knox moved in close again, his lips brushing her jaw. "And I love you, sweetheart."

"I love you, too." Jana slid her hands up his chest and behind his neck.

"That's good to hear," he kissed the edge of her mouth, "because it looks like you're gonna be my wife."

Jana laughed.

"And I'm hoping that my fiancée will read the rest of her book to me tonight."

"Oh?" She smiled. "Is that your way of getting an invite into the house?"

"Whatever it takes."

Jana smirked. "Then come on in, Mr. Prosper." She led him by the hand inside. They settled on the couch together, and she nestled against Knox's side. She opened her laptop to read the last couple of chapters.

Knox rested his chin on top of her head, and randomly stole kisses.

"The end," she said softly.

Knox's fingers skimmed down her arm. "I loved it."

Jana tilted her head so she could meet his gaze. "You're just being sweet."

"I am being sweet," he said, his green eyes focused on her, "but I also loved the story. You have a gift with words, Jana."

Her eyes stung with tears she hadn't expected. "Thanks, that means a lot."

"Pretty soon, I'm going to be known as author Jana Prosper's husband."

She laughed. "Hardly. I'll always be Knox Prosper's wife."

"I'm counting on it, sweetheart."

She slipped her arms about his neck and drew him close. She decided that whatever happened in any book she ever wrote, it would never compare to the real-life relationship with the man by her side. They may not have had the best beginning, but she was counting on the best ending.

Heather B. Moore is a four-time *USA Today* bestselling author. She writes historical thrillers under the pen name H.B. Moore; her latest thrillers include *The Killing Curse* and *Breaking Jess*. Under the name Heather B. Moore, she writes romance and women's fiction. Her newest releases include the historical novels *The Paper Daughters of Chinatown* and *Deborah: Prophetess of God*. She's also one of the coauthors of the *USA Today* bestselling series: A Timeless Romance Anthology. Heather writes speculative fiction under the pen name Jane Redd; releases include the Solstice series and *Mistress Grim*. Heather is represented by Dystel, Goderich & Bourret.

For book updates, sign up for Heather's email list: hbmoore.com/contact
Website: HBMoore.com
Facebook: Fans of H.B. Moore
Blog: MyWritersLair.blogspot.com
Instagram: @authorhbmoore
Pinterest: HeatherBMoore
Twitter: @HeatherBMoore

www.ingramcontent.com/pod-product-compliance
Lightning Source LLC
LaVergne TN
LVHW021236080526
838199LV00088B/4538